"Does He Have a Name?"

she asked. "This dashing figment of your imagination?"

"Yes. Since he's sort of a cross between Zorro and Conan the Barbarian, I call him Zonan."

"I see. A sophisticated barbarian."

"More or less."

"And who am I supposed to be?" For some reason the question made her heart start to pound.

His eyes gleamed down into hers as he answered. "Not *supposed to be.* You *are* the most beautiful woman in the room."

NORA POWERS

taught English at the college level while working on her Ph.D. A prolific writer, she is the author of some 500 pieces of children's verse, 58 short stories, 9 novels, and various newspaper articles. She has been a published author for the last twenty years and reports, "I don't even recall how I started writing, I was so young."

Dear Reader:

SILHOUETTE DESIRE is an exciting new line of contemporary romances from Silhouette Books. During the past year, many Silhouette readers have written in telling us what other types of stories they'd like to read from Silhouette, and we've kept these comments and suggestions in mind in developing SILHOUETTE DESIRE.

DESIREs feature all of the elements you like to see in a romance, plus a more sensual, provocative story. So if you want to experience all the excitement, passion and joy of falling in love, then SILHOUETTE DESIRE is for you.

Karen Solem
Editor-in-Chief
Silhouette Books

NORA POWERS
A Different Reality

Silhouette Desire
Published by Silhouette Books New York
America's Publisher of Contemporary Romance

SILHOUETTE BOOKS
300 E. 42nd St., New York, N.Y. 10017

Copyright © 1985 by Nora Powers

Distributed by Pocket Books

ISBN: 0-373-05196-4

First Silhouette Books printing March, 1985

10 9 8 7 6 5 4 3 2 1

America's Publisher of Contemporary Romance

Printed in the U.S.A.

BC91

Silhouette Books by Nora Powers

Silhouette Romance

Silhouette Desire

for John
with love

A Different
Reality

1

The small office, crisp and businesslike, made a good background for the figure seated at the shining desk with its neatly stacked piles of work. It should be clear to anyone entering here that the woman who managed this large hotel meant business.

Amber Sinclair straightened her shoulders and spoke into the phone. "Yes, Mr. Holden, that's been taken care of. All of it. I'm sure you'll find everything to your satisfaction." She grimaced and absently tugged at a wisp of red-brown hair that had escaped from her French knot. Her dark brown eyes clouded and the slim hand that held the phone began to tremble slightly as she fought for control. She had to end this conversation quickly, even if it was necessary to use a little subterfuge.

She moved the phone a little away from her mouth

as she put her plan into action. "Yes, Betsy. Send him in." There was no one else in the room, but Holden, on the other end of the line, couldn't be aware of that. She spoke into the phone again. "I'm sorry, Mr. Holden, but I really have to say good-bye now. My appointment is here."

Even this subterfuge made it difficult for her to disengage herself from her persistent caller. When finally she put the phone back in its cradle, her shoulders slumped in exhaustion. She let her head fall into her hands and sighed. This Mr. Holden was going to be a handful. And the convention that he had booked into the Merryweather Hotel was going to be a nuisance. She could feel it.

Sighing again, she got to her feet and moved to look out the window toward the river. The May sun was making outdoor Memphis look especially inviting. But she had work to do. She pulled at the bottom of her neat gray jacket, a jacket that fit a body almost too slender, and pushed again at the red-brown hair that framed her pale face. But that face wore a look of determination. She stretched, easing tired muscles, then turned back to her desk again and the stack of work that awaited her.

Sliding into her chair, she reached absently to pick up a paperweight that held an embedded piece of amber. She stared at the swirls of translucent color for a long, long moment. This piece exactly matched the color of her hair. That was why she had given in to temptation and bought it, a relatively useless thing. Her hand closed around its smoothness. It was, after all, only a collection of molecules.

That was what her science-minded parents would tell her, she knew. A collection of molecules like any other "thing" she might choose to hold in her hand. Like everything in this great machine that was the universe. There was no place for whim in the world her parents knew.

Still, she thought as her hand closed around its warm smoothness, she had wanted it and she had bought it. She was an adult now. And a paperweight could hardly hurt her. Not like . . .

Amber sighed and put the paperweight back on the desk. Buying it had probably been a mistake, a reversion to the foolish kind of longing that Andy had aroused in her. She supposed a psychiatrist would understand it perfectly—the lure Andy had held for her. She could see him still—tall and dark, with laughter-filled eyes. How Andy had laughed. Life was one big joke to him.

She pulled a stack of papers toward her. She had work to do. But Andy's ghost would not be routed. She saw him in her mind, grinning at her, as though inviting her to share another evening of fun. She picked up a pen. She would share no more of Andy's fun. Ever.

It was true that he had captivated her at first. She had been a shy, quiet girl whose parents, both high school science teachers, had so impressed her with the seriousness of this world that she rarely laughed. But with Andy she was a different person. With Andy the world became a magical place, full of excitement, full of fun. A place of enchantment, of imagination.

He was like a disease, she thought. She no longer

blamed herself for being swept off her feet. Nor did she blame her parents. They had done their best to warn her. But what use were the warnings of dry scientific minds when a girl was young and in love, when for the first time life held exuberant joy? When, as her parents had so objectively pointed out, her hormones were in charge, and not her mind. No use at all, Amber told herself sadly. For as soon as she had reached the age of consent, she'd slipped away to marry Andy and ensure that their happiness would last forever.

Amber swallowed over the lump in her throat. It hadn't lasted, of course. Happiness never did. But it hadn't even settled into contentment. At first she'd been ecstatic, fixing up their little apartment, cooking fancy dinners for Andy, following him into the little bedroom.

Amber shuddered. It was painfully easy to remember the nights she had huddled under piles of blankets because Andy had neglected to pay the electric bill, the pitiful excuses she had offered the landlord when he demanded his overdue rent. It was that kind of thing, finally, the knowledge that any day they might be thrown into the street, that had driven her to get the job as secretary in a hotel. Andy had cheerfully agreed. He had no pride about such things. She could pay the bills if she was worried about them.

She'd puzzled over his attitude for a long time. What was it that made him the way he was? He wasn't a bad person, not overtly cruel. Nothing like that. Just selfish. He didn't see any reason for paying bills on time. He wasn't affected by the embarrassment, the inconvenience, the calls from collection agencies. He paid his bills only at the last possible moment, and sometimes not even then. Sometimes he chose to move on instead. After that first year there had been a succession of different apartments in different towns.

She was not sure, now, why she had stayed with him for so long. It was true that he was all she had. Her parents had more or less washed their hands of her after her marriage. Andy was all she had and she clung to him. She took care of him. She worked hard at the jobs she always managed to land in various hotels. Over time she had advanced and with each new job she worked her way a little higher on the ladder of hotel management. In that way she achieved a kind of contentment.

Until the day she came home from work early with the flu and found Andy packing again. He had decided to see yet another new town and he expected her to go with him. Just like that he expected her to give up her job one more time. She hadn't been able to do it.

Strange, Amber thought, that his leaving had not been more painful. But perhaps it was only habit that had been holding them together. She had not missed Andy since the day he'd moved out, except in the sense that she no longer had to worry about him and what problems he might cause her, no longer had to pay the bills that he so unconcernedly ran up.

And then had come the chance at this job in Memphis—and a fresh start. Her parents had wanted to become friendly again after the divorce, but she could not forget the years of silence, or bear their

I-told-you-so looks. Yes, it was far better to be away from them for a while, to concentrate on her career. She picked up a letter and began to read.

"Mrs. Sinclair?" The door to the outer office opened far enough to admit a head graced with bouncy yellow curls.

"Yes, Betsy?"

The young secretary came in and shut the door behind her. She was wearing a proper business suit, but nothing could subdue Betsy's vitality. "I've checked all the arrangements. Did that Mr. Holden have any last-minute changes?"

Amber shook her head. "No, he just wanted to check on things." She frowned slightly.

Betsy's quick smile was sympathetic. "Don't worry, Mrs. Sinclair. Most of them are really nice people."

Amber indicated a chair. "Sit down a minute, Betsy. Tell me what you know about this convention."

Betsy dropped gracefully into the chair. "It's a lot of fun. They held it here last year, too. It's called the Mem-Con. For Memphis, you see. I only worked part-time then. I went to some of the things."

Amber smiled. Sometimes Betsy seemed about eight years old. But there was nothing childish about her capacity for hard work. "Go on."

"Science fiction conventions are kind of different. I mean, they talk about wild ideas and, well, it's so exciting. Thinking about other worlds and stuff like that."

Amber didn't find it exciting at all. She found the whole thing rather distressing. Conventions were always troublesome. People drank too much; the halls got noisy. There was always something going on, something certain to be annoying to the other guests. "What kind of people come to a thing like this?"

Betsy's eyes sparkled. "Oh, all kinds. College professors, students, bookstore owners, writers, artists; just ordinary readers, too, I guess. I had a real good time."

Amber shook her head. "Were they noisy?"

"Not really. Oh, we had a few complaints about the costumes."

"Costumes?" Amber felt a headache coming on.

"Yeah, some of them come in costume. Dress up like their favorite characters. It's a lot of fun."

Amber rubbed absently at her temples, trying to reduce the tension left there by Mr. Holden. What Betsy was telling her did very little to help.

"Oh, let me see. They wear all kinds of things. Ah, last year there was a guy dressed like Conan the Barbarian. He had long hair and a beard. Of course, Conan doesn't have a beard." Betsy grinned. "But this guy didn't care about that. He had a red handkerchief around his head, and a towel around his waist, with a rubber chicken hanging on his belt, and sandals."

Amber waited, trying to visualize it all. Horrified pictures of complaining guests rose in her mind. "You mean that's *all* he wore?"

Betsy giggled. "Well, they say he had gym shorts under the towel. I wasn't there when he stood on his head." She giggled. "He gave one of the female security guards a real start. She was standing there when the elevator door opened."

Betsy's smile was pure mischief, but her words were serious. "I sort of told the guards what to expect this year. So they don't get uptight."

Amber nodded absently. Her mind was still focused on the picture Betsy had given her. And her headache was growing by the minute.

"And there was a woman in a beautiful long gown; brocade, I think, with sleeves that hung all the way to the floor. She said it was copied from one in the Middle Ages. She was from the SCA."

Amber sighed; there was no doubt about it. Now she was fighting a full-blown headache. "And what is that?"

"It's the Society for Creative . . . Anachronisms." Betsy hesitated over the long word. "They wear medieval costumes and fight with swords and armor."

"Swords and armor," Amber repeated dully. She was beginning to wish she had never left Chicago. Even her parents' attitude was preferable to this.

"You'll see," Betsy went on cheerfully. "They'll be giving a demonstration on Saturday. Out on the side lawn."

"A demonstration with swords?"

Betsy shrugged her slim shoulders. "No need to worry. The swords are made of wood." She frowned. "I think they said rattan. But they make a nice noise."

"Be sure to give these people the name and number of a nearby medical center," Amber said dryly.

Betsy burst into delighted laughter. "Oh, I don't think they'll need that. But I'll have it ready." She paused.

Amber knew that look. Betsy was debating about telling her something more. "What is it?" she asked.

The first time she'd ignored that look she'd run into a woman walking a Great Dane down the hall and only the fact that Betsy had been in the office when she went to call Security had saved her from making a serious mistake. For the woman with the Great Dane was the sister of the owner's friend, and had the right to keep *anything* in her room.

So now Amber repeated, "What else should I know?"

"Well, there's a game they play, called Assassin." Betsy hesitated, then grinned apologetically. "I used to go with this fellow. He was really into science fiction and he told me all this stuff. This game started out as something called KAOS—killing as organized sport."

Amber glanced sharply at the young secretary and Betsy hurried on. "They draw names, the people who are playing. And each one has one particular person to 'kill.' They have rubber daggers to do it with. And they have to get their particular person when he can't defend himself. The 'victims' have water pistols for defense, filled with cheap perfume."

Amber shook her head, then winced, and was forcefully reminded of her headache by a sharp jab of pain. "I can't believe that Mr. Sampson allowed this kind of thing." She had only seen Mr. Sampson once, before he moved on to a bigger and better job. But he had not seemed a frivolous sort of man.

Betsy nodded. "I know it seems funny. But he did." Her voice dropped and she giggled again. "In fact, he went to the masquerade. So did I. I wore this . . ."

She stopped, aware from the look on her employer's face that she'd better not digress too far. "Well, Mr. Sampson went as a pirate, with an eye patch and a real sword." She giggled for the third time. "He looked pretty scary, too."

Betsy straightened primly. "I did wonder about using those squirt guns in the halls." Her small nose wrinkled delicately. "That perfume was just awful. But Mr. Sampson said they had the owner's approval. That he liked science fiction, too."

Amber sighed. "Do you remember this Mr. Holden —Everett Holden?"

Betsy shook her head, blonde curls bouncing. "No, I don't remember the name." She frowned. "I don't like the way he talks, though. I'm afraid he fancies himself something of a ladies' man. In fact"—Betsy hesitated and a flush spread over her cheeks—"I'd look out for him if I were you. If he weren't a guest, I'd have told him where to go!"

Betsy's bristling indignation brought a small smile to Amber's lips. "Yes, Betsy. I got that message, too. But you're right about one thing. We work here and Mr. Holden is a guest, so we're going to have to keep cool and polite."

Betsy nodded. "I'll try, but it isn't going to be easy. Too bad he isn't just some ordinary guy." She grinned. "I know how to get rid of one of them real quick."

She got to her feet and went to the door, pausing with her hand on the knob. "Don't you worry, Mrs. Sinclair, we'll manage just fine. Maybe even teach that Mr. Holden a lesson."

Amber smiled dryly. "I doubt we can do that, Betsy, though the man's clearly in need of one." She glanced at her watch. "Almost five. It'll soon be time for you to leave."

Betsy frowned and threw a glance at the stack of letters on the desk. "I'll be glad to stay and help."

"No, Betsy." This time Amber remembered not to shake her head, which was now thudding dully. "That's all right. You just go on home."

Betsy frowned and her expression was grave. "You shouldn't work so hard, Mrs. Sinclair. Work's okay, but you need a little fun, too."

The word pierced like a knife, but Amber kept the pain from her face and smiled. "I'm fine, Betsy. You run along. There'll be a lot to do tomorrow."

"Okay." Betsy's expression was not happy, but she knew when she was beaten. "See you then."

As the door closed behind her secretary Amber reached for the top letter on the pile. She really didn't have to stay here and work overtime. There wasn't that much to be done. But the thought of going back to her suite wasn't particularly inviting. Here, at least, there was something to distract her mind.

She sighed and the letter slipped from her fingers. The suite went with the job and she was grateful for that. She had salvaged very little from those years of marriage. There had been very little to salvage. Aside from the few pieces of clothing she needed for her job, she had spent nothing on herself. The rest of her income had gone for the rent and the groceries and for paying Andy's bills.

She leaned back in the chair and stared unseeing

across the room. It seemed incredible now that she had taken care of him for so long. Who was doing that now? she wondered, laughter bitter on her lips. Someone was, she was sure. Some woman. Andy had always been able to find a woman willing to believe in him. For a little while, at least. And when that one was gone, why, he would simply shrug and find another.

Intangibles like love had very little meaning for Andy. Sitting there in the silent office, she relived that shattering afternoon. Stumbling home from work with a fever of 102, she had thought with longing of the comfort of her bed. She had opened the door, shrugged out of her coat, dropped her purse, and made a beeline for the bedroom and the bed.

And then she had seen them, the boxes, the clothes dragged out of the closets. After hearing Andy's cavalier explanation, watching him creating more disorder, she had known finally and completely that she couldn't go with him. She simply could not face starting over in a new place.

Her illness was forgotten as Amber made her decision. Perhaps it had already been made; perhaps this was just the last straw. But whatever the reason, she knew with absolute certainty that it was time for Andy to make a choice. Either he stayed with her and made an effort to put their marriage back on track, or he went on without her.

She told him so clearly and calmly, but she couldn't quite stem her bitter laughter at his aggrieved "But I like new places, honey. You know that." As usual, he gave no thought at all to what *she* liked. And as usual, his wanderlust was stronger than his feelings for her.

With a shudder Amber recalled herself to the present. That was all behind her now. The hotel suite wasn't very homelike, though she had added a plant or two, but her bank account was growing steadily. When she had enough saved, she would rent a nice place and furnish it comfortably. But first she had to have some money put away for a rainy day, a luxury she had never been able to afford with Andy.

She looked at her watch and pushed back her chair. Enough. It was time to go have some soup and crackers, watch a little TV, and go to bed. She would need her strength tomorrow.

2

~~~~~~~~~

The next afternoon, returning from a quick lunch in the hotel dining room, Amber passed the registration center for the convention. They had set aside several conference rooms, one of which was to be called the Hucksters' Room. The table for registration had been set up outside that door. Looking around, Amber congratulated herself: everything was in order. All the convention rooms were located in the same area. She ran over the list in her mind. The Hucksters' Room, which apparently sold items related to science fiction, an art gallery, a meeting room. She paused in her thoughts. The video room—where science fiction movies played continuously—was not so close to this area, nor was the suite where the sponsoring organization dispensed free soft drinks and beer. Her nose wrinkled distastefully at the thought of guests with access to free alcohol. Well, at least Mr. Holden should be satisfied. She didn't see how he could have gotten better accommodations for his convention.

She took a turn through the Hucksters' Room. The many tables were covered with paperbacks, comic books, calendars, cards, figures of unicorns and dragons. Posters and drawings decorated the walls. It was almost like entering another world—a strange, alien world.

That feeling was heightened by the costumed guests scattered through the room. Some she could more or less recognize—a pirate was a pirate in any world, as was a medieval maiden. But others, with orange and black faces that resembled strange animals, or weird green ears and pink hair, were complete enigmas to her.

She found herself searching, rather fearfully, for the young towel-clad barbarian who had captured Betsy's fancy, but fortunately he was not to be seen. Perhaps, she thought hopefully, he would not put in an appearance this year. As soon as she grew aware of this hope, she knew its futility. The first rule of conventions was that anything that *could* go wrong *would* go wrong. In fact, that might be the first rule of life, too. As her parents had often told her, expect nothing and you'll be pleased with whatever you do get. She had rebelled against that philosophy once; had frantically tried to grasp happiness in both hands. She knew the pain that came from that. No, Amber Sinclair wasn't looking for happiness now. All she asked of life—and she was prepared to work very hard to get it—was a small measure of security and a little contentment.

She had reached the halfway point in her circuit of the room when she became aware that someone was watching her. An uncomfortable feeling grew in the back of her neck, a kind of prickling. She let her eyes go round the room.

They came to an abrupt halt when they met, on the other side of the room, the dark eyes of a masked stranger. For a long moment those eyes held hers before she wrenched her gaze away. Shaken, she turned to the table beside her and pretended to examine a book there. To her surprise she found that she had formed a complete picture of the man in those few seconds that their eyes had been locked together. He was wearing black tights with soft black boots, a black shirt whose full sleeves were slashed with crimson. A black cloak, crimson-lined, was thrown over his shoulder, and the sword that hung at his belt looked very real.

But it was his face she remembered most clearly—a lean dark face with a wicked-looking black beard and mustache around a firm mouth, a bold nose, and those burning black eyes showing through the holes in his black mask. If ever a man looked the part of a dashing rogue, it was the man whose eyes had rested so speculatively on her. A shudder shivered down her spine and she almost dropped the book she was holding.

Get a grip on yourself, she scolded silently. The man's just seeing what's available. She had seen that look before. She was not, after all, an unattractive woman. But she was certainly not available. Not to a man like him—someone so childish that he ran around in a costume, no matter how well it became him. There was no telling how irresponsible a man like that could be.

She put the book back with the others and headed toward the door, carefully keeping her averted eyes from that dark figure across the room.

This was going to be an unsettling weekend, she thought some minutes later as she settled down behind her desk and absently picked up her amber paperweight. She was only vaguely aware of the comfort she found in it. She had not given any thought to what it might symbolize for her. That it was beautiful was not a valid reason for her. Beauty was unimportant in the world her parents had taught her to live in. In their world of stark, scientific fact, beauty did not exist. It was an intangible, scientifically unprovable, and therefore quite useless.

She sat in silence for several minutes, striving for a sense of calm that would let her focus her mind once more on her work. This convention was even more unsettling than she had expected it to be. She mused over this for a moment. Could it be because the people reminded her so much of Andy? Certainly the world of irresponsibility that he lived in was no more like the reality she knew than were the worlds inhabited by the fanciful creatures of science fiction.

A loud rap on the door made her jump and she looked up. "Yes?" she called.

The figure that threw open the door looked as though it had come out of someone's nightmare. The helmet with its protruding horns marked the man as some kind of Viking. His rough tunic and trousers didn't hide a stomach that was definitely unwarrior-like, but the small eyes sunk deep behind heavy cheeks certainly gave him the look of a predator.

"Mrs. Sinclair. At last I get to meet the elusive little lady."

Amber recognized the voice at once. She was incapable of smiling, but she did manage to say calmly, "Hello, Mr. Holden."

Behind him, she could see Betsy's fatalistic shrug and knew that the young secretary had done her best to keep the man out. "How can I help you today?" She regretted even that formally phrased request as the man advanced into the room.

"Just wanted to see the pretty lady I've been talking to on the phone."

Amber suppressed a sigh as he settled his bulk into a chair. "I think you'll find everything in perfect order for your convention," she said.

Holden shrugged. "I expect so, little lady."

His eyes moved over her and for a miserable minute she wondered if even armor would make her feel secure from that salacious glance.

He leaned forward in his chair, his protruding stomach straining against his rough tunic. Amber steeled herself for yet more fulsome flattery. The phone rang sharply. With a muttered "excuse me" she picked it up.

"Five minutes?" Betsy said. "Then the old emergency trick?"

Amber kept her voice strictly businesslike. "Yes, Mr. Carpenter. That should be fine."

As she replaced the phone in its cradle she mentally

braced herself. Five minutes wasn't such a long time. She could stand anything for five minutes. She turned to Everett Holden. "Everything is ready, Mr. Holden. I've checked it all out. I'm sure you'll be pleased with the arrangements."

"If you made them, I will be."

Amber allowed herself only one pained thought: How could such a man think himself attractive to women? Then she set herself to giving him the most detailed descriptions, up to and including the seating capacities of the various rooms set aside for convention use. With admirable finesse she overrode Holden's every attempt to lead the conversation into other, more personal channels until finally the interminable five minutes had passed. As prearranged, Betsy's welcome knock sounded on the door, and Amber called, "Come in."

Betsy looked properly disturbed. "I'm sorry to interrupt," she said, with an apologetic glance at the man in the chair. "But there's an emergency. It's Mrs. Hegemy."

Amber rose swiftly. "I'll go right away." She turned to Holden. "Mrs. Hegemy is one of our problem guests. But an important one."

Holden heaved his bulk out of the chair. "I'll go with you."

"Oh, no, you can't!" The words escaped before she could stop them.

"Why not?"

"It's . . . it's Mrs. Hegemy," she improvised. "She hates men. Just the sight of one sends her off. No, I'll have to go alone. Betsy will show you out."

Without waiting for a reply, she raced out the door and down the corridor to the stairs. One quick look showed her that Betsy had managed to delay Holden and she pushed open the door and hurried up the stairs to the safety of her suite.

Shaking like a leaf, she sank down on the bed and tried to relax. By now she ought to have learned not to be so upset by men like Holden, she told herself. She wasn't really afraid of the man. There was more to this than simple fear. It must be because in some obscure way he reminded her of Andy. Not in his looks. Andy was an attractive man. And not in his approach. Andy was much smoother.

The hands she was trying to relax turned suddenly into fists. That was it! She had found his resemblance to Andy. Everett Holden was a user. Pure and simple. And she wanted to stay as far away from users as possible. She glanced at her watch and reached for the phone. There was work to be done in the office.

Ten minutes later she was heading toward the Hucksters' Room again. She had decided to make the return trip to her office by a roundabout route. The last thing she wanted Holden to know was the location of her suite, or even that she lived in the hotel.

Betsy had said he was not around the office and if Amber ran into him anywhere else she had her stories ready. One about the imaginary Mrs. Hegemy's problem sink and one about an important phone call, which she could be expecting at any hour if Holden kept after her.

A DIFFERENT REALITY

The Hucksters' Room was to her right and she found herself going in, her eyes searching the tables. But, she realized with a sense of shock as disappointment registered in her mind, she was not looking for Everett Holden in order to avoid him. She was looking for a tall dark figure in black.

This was ridiculous, she told herself. The dark stranger might look attractive, all dressed up in his fancy costume. Undeniably, he was lean and trim. But up close she would probably discover that he had a weak chin and shifty eyes.

She finished her circuit of the room and moved on toward her office. Then she saw him. He was sitting on a couch by the circular stairs that led down to the first floor, his long lean legs stretched nonchalantly before him. His eyes burned into her and she felt herself flushing scarlet as she pulled her gaze away and hurried on down the stairs.

She sighed as she reached her office and managed a shaky smile for Betsy before she closed the door behind her with a sense of relief. Sinking into her chair, she pulled a pile of papers toward her and noticed with dismay that her hand was trembling.

She frowned. This was too much. It was bad enough having Holden after her. He was annoying, but she knew she could handle him. This dark stranger was another story. He was almost sinister in his attractiveness. She reminded herself again that without his fancy costume he was probably nondescript. But those burning eyes were not part of any costume.

She had just picked up the top letter and begun to

read when a tap sounded on the door and Betsy opened it. "There's someone here to see you, Mrs. Sinclair."

"Who . . . ?" Amber began. And then Betsy stepped aside and he filled the doorway. Up close his bearded chin had a thrust to it that belied any possible weakness and his eyes were decidedly not shifty, but warm and friendly. She noted absently that he had removed the black scarf that had served him as a mask.

Betsy was plainly smitten with the man; she stood there staring for a moment before she remembered to turn back to her desk.

Amber swallowed hastily. "I'm sorry," she said, her voice as cold as she could make it when the rest of her body seemed suddenly to have burst into flame, "but I don't believe you have any business with me."

He pulled the door shut behind him and covered the space to her desk in three long strides. "Are you Amber Sinclair?"

"Yes." The way he said her name almost unnerved her. She braced herself mentally.

"Then you're just the person I want to see." He stuck out a black-gloved hand. "Kerr Corrigan. I'm in charge of next year's convention arrangements."

She had no choice then but to capitulate as gracefully as possible. She took the hand he had offered her, shook it briefly, but was still very much aware of its warmth and strength. She motioned to a chair. "Won't you sit down?"

He sank into the chair with catlike grace and part of her mind noted how naturally his hand went to adjust the sword that hung at his hip. For some reason, it didn't look at all silly there.

"Now then," he began. "I like what I've seen of this year's arrangements, but I have a few questions and maybe a suggestion or two."

Amber listened carefully, trying her best to be businesslike. But the man seemed to generate sexual excitement. No man had affected her like this since she'd first met Andy. That made the stranger even more dangerous to her.

"So," he finished. "That's about it. Have you any questions?"

She wet suddenly dry lips. "I understand there's a game. Assassin, I believe it's called."

He nodded.

"You people must understand that I can't have the hotel's other guests upset. Or sprayed by cheap perfume. Which, I understand, is carried around in water pistols." Her tone conveyed her disgust at this kind of juvenile behavior.

He smiled, showing white teeth against his dark mustache and beard. "Unless one of your guests attacks someone with a rubber dagger they aren't likely to be 'shot.' The rules of the game don't allow for the 'victims' to go around indiscriminately 'killing' everyone they see. An attempt has to be made on them before they can defend themselves."

Amber felt that she had to nod in agreement. What he said made perfect sense. Still, her years in the business had shown her that convention guests meant more trouble than any other kind.

His eyes met hers again and in an effort to stop the

blush she felt coming, she let her eyes drop to his sword. And that gave her something else to say.

"I am also somewhat concerned about the costume ball." She gestured toward his sword. "So many weapons floating around. There's potential for trouble there."

He nodded calmly, but she noticed that his hand went almost protectively to the sword at his side. "I can sympathize with your concern. This is a big place and you have a lot of guests to look out for."

His understanding pleased her more than it should have. "Do you suppose you could eliminate the carrying of weapons?" she asked hopefully.

He frowned, bringing together heavy black brows. "I'm afraid not. Weapons are part of the fun."

Her face registered her disbelief.

"It's true," he said. "But listen, don't worry about the weapons. I have the perfect answer for you."

Her heart seemed to vibrate and she found to her surprise that she wanted to touch him, wanted to touch this perfect stranger. She clasped her hands firmly together in her lap and forced her lips to form the words "you do?"

"Yes. You must come to the ball yourself."

The words of refusal sprang automatically to her lips. "I can't. I've no costume, for one thing. And having a kind of 'policewoman' around would certainly not be appreciated." She was momentarily surprised to realize that some crazy part of her actually wanted to attend this childish ball.

"No problem," he said, rising easily to his feet. "I'll

see that you have a costume. And a registration badge. You can just be one of the guests."

"But . . ." she began again.

"Yes, that's certainly the way to do it," he went on cheerfully. "That way you can see for yourself that we're just ordinary people having a good time."

He moved toward the door, where he turned to give her one last burning look from eyes that seemed to reach into her very depths. "I'll have your costume sent to the office here. I look forward to seeing you this evening."

"But I . . ." Her words fell into empty air. Kerr Corrigan had closed the door softly behind him. For a moment Amber considered jumping to her feet and racing after him. How could she possibly go to a masquerade ball? That was sheer childishness.

But for some reason she didn't move. His argument had been logical. If she was at the ball herself, she could keep an eye on things—and a costume would preserve her anonymity. Still . . .

Her hand stole out to close around the amber paperweight again. A furrow creasing between her brows, she gazed down at it. She didn't think of it as a talisman or a good-luck piece. She didn't believe in luck.

She let her thoughts center on the image of Kerr Corrigan. There was no sense in denying that he was an extremely attractive man. His chin was not weak, but strong and determined. His eyes were not shifty, but friendly and . . . She paused. The proper word was *alluring*. And his body . . . His body was trim and firm, an athlete's body, showed off to perfection by the black tights and the shirt with the theatrical red-slashed sleeves, a body that made a woman's breath catch in her throat. She could see every article of his costume with crystal clarity, including the sword, which should have made him look silly and somehow didn't.

Everett Holden, now, in contrast, looked utterly ridiculous, running around in a Viking outfit that revealed all his worst physical features. But Kerr . . . She didn't even notice that she had begun to think of him by his first name. Kerr's looks fit his costume.

She put the paperweight down and reached for her mail. What kind of costume would he pick for her? she wondered. With a sigh she forced herself to go back to work. She would find that out soon enough.

3

~~~~~~~~~~~~~~~~~

The box with the costume in it arrived in midafternoon, carried in by a grinning and obviously curious Betsy. But Amber refused to be lured away from her work and a disappointed Betsy had to go back to her desk without seeing what the mysterious box contained. Through the rest of the afternoon it sat there, supposedly ignored.

Five o'clock came finally, Betsy left, though not without several trips to the door, and Amber picked up the box and hurried off to her suite. Her fingers trembled as she pulled the box open and began to lift out the items it contained. A black shirt, its sleeves slashed with crimson, black tights, soft black boots, a crimson-lined black cloak. The costume was identical to Kerr Corrigan's. She smiled as she lifted the last item from the box—a black scarf with holes in it for her eyes. The only thing lacking was a sword.

She wasn't sure how to take this omission. Had he thought her unable to handle a sword? Or was he merely considering her aversion to weapons? There was no way to tell.

She stripped off her suit and turned toward the shower. She realized then that she was anxious to see herself in these clothes and she felt foolish for enjoying such a thing. But it was only sensible, she told herself firmly, for her to be on hand at the masquerade. What better way to be sure that things were under control than to be right there?

Coming out of the shower, she toweled herself dry and returned to the bedroom and the costume so invitingly spread out on the bed. It was still early, but she began to dress anyway. One more costumed figure in the halls would hardly be noticed.

She pulled the tights up over her panties. They were certainly black enough. She hooked her bra and dropped the shirt over her head, liking the soft feel of it. The body of the shirt was almost form-fitting and she wondered how Kerr had guessed the right size. She belted it over the tights and slipped on the boots before buttoning the voluminous sleeves with their crimson inserts.

The costume was very theatrical. She moved over to look at herself in the mirror. Surprise made her gasp. The masculine costume accented her femininity. In her business suits she was cool and remote, but in this costume . . . The tights clung to her legs and rounded hips and the swell of her small breasts was clearly visible under the clinging shirt.

She eyed herself and frowned. She needed more colorful makeup than her usual pale pastels. Rummaging through her drawer, she came up with a vivid-colored lipstick and a pot of rouge. A few minutes later, having added eye shadow and mascara, all leftovers from her time with Andy, she felt like a different woman.

For one long moment she wished for a sword to hang at her hip. What would it feel like to be armed? She shook her head. That was not something she meant to find out. She was already going a little far appearing in this costume, which, in spite of the fact that it covered her completely, made her feel almost naked. Thank goodness for the cloak.

Eyeing herself again, she realized that something was still wrong. Her hair, in its usual French knot, just didn't look right with this outfit. Hurriedly she pulled out the hairpins and let it fall loose. Yes, that was better. As she fastened the cloak around her shoulders, a nervous giggle rose up in her throat. Silly as she felt, she was determined to go through with this thing.

For a moment she could see her parents, see the dire expressions of disapproval on their faces if they saw her about to behave so foolishly. She shrugged. She wasn't doing this for fun, she told their imaginary faces. It was part of her job.

She ran the hairbrush through her hair, allowing herself to savor its softness under her fingers. Andy had always liked her hair. Her expression hardened. Andy was no longer part of her life. Someday she would find a sound, sensible man.

She pushed the thought of Andy away—it was growing easier and easier to do. All the hurt had left long ago. There was still some anger, but even that had dissipated. Probably Andy couldn't help what he was.

Picking up the key to her room, she paused, momentarily at a loss. There was no place in this costume to put anything. Finally she reached inside the shirt's V neck and deposited the key between her breasts. Her bra would keep it secure there. With a last look around, she went out and closed the door behind her.

The halls were crowded with masqueraders as she made her way toward the ballroom. Every kind of creature known to humankind, and many not, laughed and cavorted around her. Amber tried to keep the distaste she was feeling off her face; she had never realized that there were so many people like Andy, so many foolish, uncaring juveniles with no thought for tomorrow. But there were certainly plenty of them here.

Passing the suite set aside for the organization sponsoring the convention, she hesitated. Wall-to-wall people packed the room. To Amber's searching eyes it appeared that every hand held a glass of beer. Her gaze went back to the little kitchen area and she noted with relief that though the soft drinks were free for the taking a sensible-looking man was passing out the beer. Presumably he would keep it from anyone underage.

A hand came to rest against her hip and Amber started, whirling to face the man who had touched her so familiarly. But there was no one there. Or rather, there were so many people around her that it was impossible to tell who had been the guilty one. No one seemed to even notice her searching glance. With a silent shudder Amber moved on, away from the crowd.

For a moment, moving on toward the lobby, she considered giving the whole thing up and going back to her suite, but she dismissed that idea as cowardly. It was her job to see that nothing went wrong during this convention. It was her job to attend this masquerade. Pushing thoughts of her parents out of her mind, she hurried on.

The Hucksters' Room was alive with convention-eers, too. Without thinking, Amber slipped in. What was it about this stuff that so fascinated people? she wondered as she paced up one aisle and down the next. Images of horrible aliens, of faster-than-light spaceships, of crude barbarian warriors, flashed through her mind. She knew no more of science fiction than that. Her parents had encouraged her to read non-fiction. Books that revealed the universe as a great machine. And didn't try to hide the facts.

How could people spend so much time reading about worlds that never had and never would exist? she asked herself. She knew the answer, of course. Like Andy, these people were escapists. Like Andy, they couldn't handle life in the "real" world, so they escaped to other, more fantastic ones.

Amber realized suddenly that her eyes had just swept the room for the third time and *he* wasn't in it. She had known that after the first search. Kerr would stand out in any gathering. Even here in the costumed crowd she was sure she could spot him.

With a sigh she turned back toward the door. She wasn't supposed to be thinking about Kerr. That wasn't why she was in this room—to look for him. Not at all. She was just checking to see that everything was running smoothly.

A glance at her watch told her the masquerade was still more than an hour off. Excitement had kept her from eating her usual dinner of soup and crackers. Maybe she should go to the dining room and get herself a sandwich. She debated briefly; she really wasn't hungry, but she had to pass the time in some way.

She frowned, trying to remember all the assigned rooms. The one set aside for the art gallery was just down the hall. She would browse there first.

The gallery wasn't crowded, she saw thankfully as she tried to focus her attention on the art. Her costume was making some people turn to look at her and once more she was glad of her mask.

She stared unseeing at the delicate drawings before her for several minutes before she really focused on them. Baby dragons. Cute, cuddly, little *baby* dragons. In Amber's mind, dragons breathed fire and inspired terror. They didn't look like fat, cherubic babies a person would like to hold. And they certainly didn't sit around drinking tea!

Conscious of someone coming closer to her, she moved on. In sharp contrast to the whimsical dragons, the next display featured glossy photolike paintings in bright sharp colors. Amber felt herself blushing slightly. One painting showed a female warrior. At least, Amber assumed it was a woman, since, though her head was in a helmet of leather, one breast was bared. With a moue of distaste, she moved on. She would take the dragons any day. At least they had some charm. What woman would ever want to go around looking like that?

The next table held an array of cartoons, originals it seemed. One showed a wizard with his pet on a leash—a Pegasus flying above his head. Amber tried to remember the story of the winged horse, but she couldn't. Her parents had frowned on the reading of mythology. It was too fanciful for their tastes, so her only exposure to it had been in high school.

Propped against the wall behind the cartoons were several colored prints of the flying horse. Amber's eyes kept going back to one of them. The great white horse was outlined against a delicate blue sky; the feathers of his huge wings seemed fragile and ethereal. For a long time she stood looking at the print, wondering why the artist had seen the great horse in that particular way.

What made it seem so beautiful to the mind that had conceived it? For it was beauty that Amber saw—in the fragile-looking legs, in the outstretched wings. A beauty that made her want, somehow, to cry. How she would like to hang that picture in the living room of her new home.

She turned away suddenly. Winged horse, indeed! She'd be far better off with a pleasant landscape or a still life. Something like that would be much more in keeping with her life-style.

"Hello," said a voice behind her, *his* voice.

The soft greeting brought her to a trembling halt. She had to lick her dry lips twice before she could turn and reply. "Hello, Kerr." He was wearing his costume, the one like hers, and again the dark scarf covered the upper half of his face.

Color flooded her cheeks as she realized she had used his first name. But he appeared not to notice.

"Admiring the art?" he asked.

She nodded. "Some of it." Unconsciously her gaze went back to the female warrior.

He chuckled. "I don't care much for that myself," he said. "My taste in women runs to Frazetta, or Boris."

Amber, trying to concentrate on his words, was shocked to realize how overwhelmed she was by the man's physical presence. There was no denying his attraction for her. Every cell in her body reminded her of it. "Who . . . who are they?" she asked.

For a moment he let his surprise show, then he replied politely. "Frank Frazetta and Boris Vallejo. They're well-known science-fiction artists. Frazetta's women are very earthy," he continued, as though he were describing the weather. "And well-fleshed."

His glance slid over her body briefly, then returned

to her face. "A little too well-fleshed for my taste. Boris's women are more to my liking. Nicely rounded and feminine, but not quite as fleshy as Frazetta's."

Amber nodded. "I see." She didn't, however. In spite of his explanations, she had only a vague idea of what he meant.

"Which of these do you like best?" he asked suddenly.

She answered without thinking. "There. The Pegasus. With the blue background."

He examined it for several moments before he replied. "Yes. I like it, too. It gives me a sense of . . . freedom. Beauty and freedom."

Amber stared at the picture. Was that why she liked it? Did the winged horse represent freedom to her? But it couldn't. Freedom was an illusion. A figment of the imagination. The great machine that was the universe rolled inexorably on. Freedom was not only an *illusion*, it was a *delusion*. One that no sensible person took much stock in.

Still, she found herself asking, "Do you know the story of Pegasus?"

"Yes." His dark eyes regarded her seriously and she experienced such a rush of emotion that for a moment she almost felt as though *she* could fly. She tried to jerk herself back to reality. "Will you tell it to me?"

"Yes. Of course. According to Greek legend, Pegasus sprang from the blood of the Gorgon when Perseus killed her. A mountain spring beloved of the poets—Hippocrene—is said to have sprung up where his hoof hit the earth. More than anything in this world

Bellerophon wanted to tame the wonderful steed and Athena gave him a golden bridle to do it with. The bridle did the trick and Pegasus was his. Together they did some great deeds, slaying the monstrous Chimaera and helping to conquer several nations. Finally Bellerophon married a king's daughter."

"A happy ending," Amber murmured, unaware of the wistfulness in her voice. It made the man beside her look down with an expression of puzzlement on his face.

"I'm afraid not," he said softly. "Oh, the story says Bellerophon lived happily for some time. But then he grew restless and his ambition got the best of him."

Amber looked up into the bearded face so near her own. "What happened?"

"'He thought thoughts too great for man.' The Greek gods didn't care for that sort of thing, as he should have known. He tried to ride Pegasus up to Mount Olympus. He had some idea of joining the gods there. But the winged horse knew better. He threw his rider and took refuge in Zeus's heavenly stable, becoming one of his foremost mounts, the one who brought him the thunder and lightning."

Amber sighed. "The horse went to Olympus without the man. And what happened to Bellerophon after that?"

"Like all the Greeks who defied the gods he came to a bad end, wandering the earth alone and forsaken until he finally died."

Amber sighed again. "That horse shouldn't be white," she said suddenly. "Or beautiful."

"Why not?" he asked, his voice serious.

"He doesn't represent freedom, or imagination," she said softly, her hands clenching at her sides. "At least, not exactly. He represents happiness, an illusion, attainment of the impossible. He should be ugly—to warn humanity of the perils of wanting too much, of daring too much."

She stopped suddenly, uncomfortably aware of the intensity of her tone, of the things about herself that she was revealing.

"Perhaps," Kerr said, his fingers light on her shoulder, sending shocks of warmth through her body. "But the searching itself—wanting and daring—can bring its own happiness." He smiled gently. "But this conversation is getting very philosophical. Too much so for a night like this. Shall we move on?"

She nodded, easing her shoulder out from under the grasp of his fingers and realizing how reluctant she was to do so.

They moved on to the next table and paused there, before some ceramic dragons. Again these were not ferocious beings, but whimsical and roly-poly creatures. "What's happened to the dragons?" she asked, more for something to say, some way to take her thoughts off the feelings he was raising in her, than because she really cared to know.

"Happened to them?" he asked.

"Yes. Well, I mean, the dragons I used to read about were horrible creatures. Nothing like these . . . babies." The word caused a rush of feeling through her. No one, not even Andy—least of all Andy, she thought with some bitterness—knew how much she wanted a child, a child to hold and to love.

"I'm not too sure when it started," he said thoughtfully. "McCaffrey has made dragons more . . ." He chuckled. "More human, I guess, is the way to say it. Of course, there was that song "Puff the Magic Dragon." And Dickson's *The Dragon and the George.*"

He shrugged. "Maybe it was just something in the air. Science fiction and fantasy writers are always exploring possibilities. I guess someone had to eventually come up with the idea of the dragon as friend."

Amber nodded. She didn't understand what drew people to this kind of reading material. The real world was horrifying enough with its greed and hate, wars and disasters of every kind. Why should anyone want to create worlds of monsters and villains even more horrible than what already existed? Wasn't this life already plagued with enough misery and misfortune?

She looked up at Kerr, meaning to say as much, but the look on his face paralyzed her tongue. His dark eyes, boring into hers, made her uneasy.

But there was something in her that refused to ignore the burning gaze of the tall dark man beside her. It was just that costume, she told herself. His costume appealed to some primeval part of her that still insisted that strong, virile men were the most desirable for a woman who wanted to assure her continued existence in a hazardous world.

Her mind presented her with a quick picture of Kerr, his beard and hair longer and tangled, his chest bare and his legs darkly matted with hair, wearing a fur loincloth and dragging a huge club. The picture should have made her laugh. Kerr's obvious sophistication made him ill-suited for such a savage role. But then she realized that the woman cowering in front of him, her long amber hair streaming over naked shoulders, had her own face.

A little quiver of disgust trembled over her. Thank goodness people no longer lived in that brutal fashion. She was perfectly capable of taking care of herself. She would cower to no man—ever.

Suddenly jerked back to reality by Kerr's fingers closing over her elbow, she shivered slightly but didn't attempt to free herself.

His chuckle was warm in her ear. "I'd offer a penny for your thoughts, but from the look on your face and the stubborn thrust of your chin, I've a feeling they wouldn't be much to my liking."

She flushed, then colored even more deeply as she realized that some part of her wanted to share that outrageous daydream with him. Stifling the impulse, she took a step toward the next table. Sharing made a woman vulnerable. And she knew very little about this man.

She looked down. "Unicorns," she said.

Kerr nodded. "Another mythical beast."

She frowned. "I remember somethiing about unicorns. Something about purity."

"Yes. A unicorn can only be tamed by an innocent maiden, a pure virgin."

"Why should anyone *want* to tame a unicorn?" she

asked, trying not to sound so serious. It had been so long since she'd engaged in any male-female give-and-take.

"To prove their purity." he suggested. "Or to have an unusual mount. One the neighbors would stare at."

This brought a small smile to her lips. "Sort of getting ahead of the Joneses?"

"Right."

His lips were full and sensuous, though she noticed that as he smiled his beard and mustache narrowed them.

With a sudden sense of surprise she realized that some part of her mind was wondering what those lips would feel like on her own. She dropped her eyes. "I . . . I don't read science fiction," she said. "I don't understand why people do. Oh, I know it's escape and all that. But I don't see how it helps. Reality is still there, waiting, when the book or movie is over."

His enigmatic smile made him look almost devilish, and even more attractive, she told herself with a sense of dismay.

"Reality is in the eye of the beholder," he whispered. "But we can discuss that later. Right now it's time for the masquerade to begin. Shall we go?"

And drawing her unresisting arm through his, he led her out of the gallery and down the hall.

4

They paused in the doorway to the ballroom, two dark masked figures clad in mysterious, romantic black. Amber was conscious that more than one pair of curious eyes were turned in their direction and it struck her with sudden force that the similarity in their costumes might lead people to believe that they were . . . a couple. She turned anxious eyes to the man who stood beside her. "I didn't think . . . Our costumes . . ."

His smile sent her heart racing. "Rather devious of me, I'm afraid."

"I don't understand." Her words were not quite true. The look of interest in his eyes wasn't hard to decipher. But she couldn't admit that interest to herself. He probably looked that way at all reasonably attractive women. Like Andy did.

"It's very simple," he said, taking her by the hand and leading her into the dimly lit room. "I sent you that costume with a nefarious purpose, I'm afraid."

"Nefarious?" She hated the telltale quiver in her voice.

"Yes. Underhanded. Tricky."

"I know what the word *means*," she replied sharply. "What I don't understand is your so-called purpose."

He bowed and kissed her hand with such grace that she didn't even feel embarrassed. What she did feel was better not thought about. "Of course," he continued. "It's really very simple. I sent you this costume . . ." His fingers moved from the hand he had tucked through his arm up to her elbow and again sudden heat moved through her body. "For several reasons. First, I can recognize you easily."

"You could do that with any costume once you saw it." She knew her voice was quivering like a schoolgirl's, but she couldn't seem to control it.

He nodded. "My second reason is really more important. Anyone seeing us will believe we're a pair and so won't approach you."

"Approach me?" She was aware that she was echoing him stupidly, but this was all moving much too fast for her.

"I believe the kids call it 'coming on to' someone," he said with that enchanting grin.

"Oh." There was nothing else she could think to say.

His fingers closed over hers again. "I don't want that

to happen because I want you all to myself. I intend to get to know you better—much better."

The pressure of his fingers on hers was turning her bones watery; she wanted to throw herself into his arms and feel the long lean length of his body against hers. This was crazy, she thought. Could putting on a costume and a mask break the restraints she had imposed on herself since Andy's departure? She didn't know. What she did know was that she felt like doing something exciting, something dangerous. And such feelings were not like her at all.

For a moment she felt a trace of fear. But, she told herself sensibly, there was no need to be afraid. She wasn't doing anything wrong. She wasn't here to have fun. She was here as part of her job. Of course, there was no rule that said she couldn't enjoy doing her job. After all, a person didn't have to be serious all the time.

A vague sense of uneasiness stole over her at the thought, which was clearly what her parents would have termed a foolish rationalization. It was their view that fun was in itself almost immoral, a waste of time that could have been put to much better use. She didn't like to believe that. Fun was not so much bad as impractical. It just didn't get a person anywhere. Conscious that Kerr's eyes were boring into hers, she realized that he had spoken to her.

"I said," he repeated. "Would you like to get to know me better?"

His eyes made his intent more than clear, but she chose to ignore the invitation shining there. "The

Merryweather Hotel does not encourage fraternizing between its staff and guests." She knew this sounded ridiculously prim and proper but she didn't care.

He shrugged. "So what? I'm not interested in the Merryweather Hotel. And *you* are evading my question."

She managed a small smile. "I'm here as part of my job, to get an idea of what goes on at this kind of thing. It was very kind of you to offer to help me. I appreciate it."

His chuckle made her face grow warm under the mask. "Well," he said, "that's better than saying 'I refuse to answer on the grounds that it might incriminate me.' Slightly better." His smile heated her blood, sent it racing through her veins. "I'm a patient man. I can wait."

She cast about in her mind for some kind of retort, but before she could come up with anything a heavy hand descended on her shoulder, immobilizing her.

"Hello there, Mrs. Sinclair."

She jerked away unconsciously as the hand touched her. Instinctively she welcomed the fact that Kerr drew protectively closer. His arm went around her and he pulled her unresisting body close against his side. The feel of him made her suddenly speechless and she could only stand silently, trembling slightly, in the shelter of his arm.

"Sorry, Holden. You've made a mistake. This isn't Mrs. Sinclair."

Holden glowered and Amber felt a sudden surge of almost hysterical laughter. The Viking clothes fit his personality better than they fit his body. His rapacious nature was evident in his whole stance. Her dislike of the man increased, if that was possible.

"What are you trying to pull?" Holden growled. The slurring of his words revealed that he had been taking full advantage of the free beer. "I'd know that hair anywhere."

Kerr shrugged and waved a vague hand at the ceiling. "I'm afraid Mrs. Sinclair's hair isn't so rich a shade as my Elizabeth's."

Disbelief and anger were mingled on Holden's face. It was not a pleasant sight. "I don't—"

"Elizabeth is my fiancée," Kerr said and his voice took on a certain threatening quality. "I dressed her this way on purpose to keep other men away." And his free hand came to rest on his sword, almost nonchalantly.

Holden blanched and even retreated an uncertain step. "Yes, okay. Sorry about the mistake. It must be the lights."

He was still scowling as he turned away and Amber bit her bottom lip to keep from laughing aloud.

"And the third reason," Kerr whispered, leaning close to her. "The third reason for dressing you like this is to protect you from characters like him."

With the warmth of his arm around her and the feel of his body against her side, she wondered who would protect her from *him*. Everett Holden was a nuisance, but he was no real danger to her. It was the men like Kerr Corrigan, like Andy, who had to be worried about. They were the ones who could hurt her.

"I think we convinced him," Kerr continued as he led her further into the dimly lit room. "At least for the time being."

Amber nodded. She'd been so conscious of Kerr, and then of Holden, that until that moment she hadn't really looked around her. Now the sight almost took her breath away. The ballroom had been transformed into a magic world. Dimly lit by lamps that constantly changed color, it bore no resemblance to the prosaic room she knew.

There were people in all kinds of costumes—from ferocious barbarians to fragile fairy maidens with shimmering wings. A knight in chain mail stood side by side with a diminutive, obviously female dragon, whose long spiked tail was draped casually over her scaly arm. A Starfleet officer walked by, in earnest conversation with an octopuslike alien whose tentacles waved realistically as he spoke. Several medieval court ladies, their long skirts and voluminous sleeves sweeping the floor, were laughing with a couple of shining robots and an alien whose startingly green face shone with eerie phosphorescence in the ballroom's dimness.

Amber raised questioning eyes. "Do each of these costumes represent a character?" she asked.

Kerr smiled. "Of one kind or another. We haven't any rules about this sort of thing. Sometimes the character is someone the person thinks up on his own. My costume, now . . ."

His smile was making her dizzy, she thought. Or maybe it was the lights, the revolving, multicolored lights that made everything in the ballroom look strange and exotic, even its ordinary furnishings.

"My costume," he continued, "represents a fantasy hero I've made up. His adventures occur only in my mind."

She disapproved of such daydreaming, such wasting of precious time, yet she was supposed to be learning about these people. "What is he like?" she asked.

He laughed softly, sheepishly. "I guess he's everything I want to be. He's handsome, dashing." He squeezed her hand. "Very attractive to women."

She was tempted to tell him that this was reality he was describing, not fantasy, but she kept silent.

"He's brave and strong. Always makes the right decisions." Again he gave her that sheepish grin. "And he always wins against the forces of evil."

Amber was unaware how much disapproval her tone conveyed as she replied, "That's fantasy, all right." Still, she was here to learn all she could. Knowing something about these people would make her better prepared to deal with them. "Does he have a name?" she asked. "This dashing figment of your imagination?"

"Yes. Since he's sort of a cross between Zorro and Conan the Barbarian, I call him Zonan."

"I see. A sophisticated barbarian."

"More or less."

"And who am I supposed to be?" For some reason the question made her heart start to pound.

His eyes gleamed down into hers as he answered.

"Not *supposed to be*. You *are* the most beautiful woman in the room."

The blood rushed to her cheeks and she felt herself trembling. Again, she longed to touch him. Careful, she told herself, be careful. This man is dangerous. "Flattery will get you nowhere," she said crisply. "I mean, what character does this costume represent?"

He hesitated. "I don't know. You'll have to invent your own. Until tonight Zonan didn't have a female companion on his adventures." He read the disbelief in her eyes and chuckled. "Oh, he had females, but only incidentally. Not as friend and companion."

For some reason this warmed her blood almost as much as his more overt compliment had. She tried to divert herself. "Are you a member of the Society for Creative Anachronism?"

"How did you know about that?" he asked, leading her skillfully through the crowd to one of the small candle-lit tables along the wall. Absently she approved of the arrangement of the ballroom.

"My secretary told me about it." She settled into a chair.

He nodded. "Yes, I belong to the local chapter. We've been trying to organize a tournament. Several of our male members would like to try jousting."

Pictures from history books flashed before Amber's eyes. "Isn't that dangerous?"

"I suppose it would be. Unfortunately—or fortunately, depending on your point of view—we haven't been able to find any horses that are willing to carry jousters. Those lances are big things."

"Smart horses, like Pegasus," Amber mumbled,

then regretted it as his twinkling eyes sought hers across the flickering candle.

"You don't think much of this kind of thing, do you?" he asked.

She shrugged. "I don't know very much about it. I'm busy with my career."

"No family?" he asked.

She felt her mouth tightening to a grim line. "No, no family."

Luckily he didn't pursue that subject.

"What do you read?" he asked, leaning toward her across the dark table.

"The classics. Hardy, Dreiser, Norris. The English philosopher Carlyle. Mostly mainstream nonfiction."

He frowned. "No wonder you see life so starkly."

"Life *is* stark," she retorted sharply. "A person should recognize that."

His face grew thoughtful. "Why? Even if it is stark—which I'm not prepared to concede—why should people recognize it? Why not pretend it's not?"

"That's foolish," she replied. "And stupid. No matter how much you try to hide it, the truth is always there."

"Truth," he said softly. "And what is truth?"

"The truth is that the world is a difficult place. We can expect that. We can expect unhappiness. That's *all* we can expect. Unless we want to be disappointed." She didn't like the sound of bitterness in her voice, but she couldn't mask it. This was not, after all, a world she had created. It was, in fact, a world she didn't much like. But it did exist.

He shook his head. "Somebody's done a real job

on you," he said, his voice holding concern. "What a gloomy way to look at life."

Annoyance crept into her voice. "My way of looking at life isn't gloomy," she insisted. "It's just realistic."

He shook his head again. "I hate to keep contradicting a lady, especially one so beautiful. But I have to. Look over there. See that couple dancing?"

She followed his gaze. "Yes, I see them."

"Okay, what do you see?"

She scowled. "I see two people dressed up in silly costumes, wasting time. One is pretending to be some kind of a maiden. The other—the one with the horned horse mask—must represent a unicorn."

He nodded. "That's what *you* see. But I see a unicorn and a maiden disporting themselves."

"But you know they aren't really . . ." she began.

"Okay. I'll play it your way. I see two people dressed in costumes that reveal some of their inner longings. Two people willing to risk living—if only briefly and in the safety of a masquerade ball—some of their inner desires."

She stared at him. "You're painting reality the way you want to see it," she accused.

His laughter was low and affectionate. "And you're not? Come on, Elizabeth-my-love. Reality is different for each and every one of us. Reality *is* how we see it."

Most of his words were lost on her. Oh, she heard them—they even registered somewhere in her mind— but what she heard, over and over in her mind, was that soft male voice saying "Elizabeth-my-love." She swallowed over a lump in her throat. "Why . . . why did you call me that?"

His eyes gleamed at her. "What?"

She didn't know if she could repeat it. "Elizabeth . . ." Her voice dropped to the merest whisper. "My-love."

He shrugged. "That's my reality. Elizabeth is Zonan's fighting companion, friend . . . and lover."

His voice sank on the last word and desire swept over her in one great enervating wave. "That's all make-believe," she stammered.

"A different reality," he corrected gently.

"But . . . but it's not true!" She felt that she was swimming in a dangerous place. She should head for shore, for safety, but instead she kept floundering on. "It's all in your mind."

He smiled and reached across the table to cover her hand with his own warm one. "We use our minds to order reality," he said softly. "You can't change mine. I can't change yours. Each person makes his own."

She could think of no rebuttal to this. It couldn't be true; she knew it couldn't be true. It was just another fantastic idea thought up by people who wanted to ignore the grimness of life. She tried to think of some way to tell him this, to make him understand, but nothing would come to her.

"Enough of this deep talk. We can get back to it later." His eyes met hers. "If you want to. But for now—let's dance."

She meant to draw back and refuse. She hadn't danced since the first years of her marriage. And this, this music sounded like a waltz. "I don't know how to waltz," she said, even as he drew her to her feet.

"It doesn't matter. I do. And I lead well. You'll learn

quickly." And as if that entirely settled the matter, he led her out onto the dance floor.

To her surprise, she picked up the one-two-three rhythm their first time around the floor. And on the second, she was able to stop concentrating on the steps and look out over his shoulder at the gaily whirling couples around them. They did look happy, she thought, as the joyous rhythm bore her along. Maybe it was the music. She remembered reading somewhere that music could have a transforming effect on people. It was only temporary, of course; another futile attempt to escape the starkness of reality. Even so, maybe it didn't hurt anything. Maybe a little escape *would* be all right.

The knight whirled by and dipped the lady dragon. Kerr's breath was warm against her ear as they, too, whirled, past robots, elves, giants, green and orange aliens, and two repulsive giant spiders whose extra legs quivered ecstatically as they turned.

Amber tried to look at them all. To keep her mind off the reactions of her body. At first Kerr had kept a little distance between them, but as she grew more accustomed to the steps, that distance had diminished until their entire bodies were in contact. The thin tights and shirts they both wore could not keep her from feeling the heat of his body and she became aware of a growing feeling within herself.

Once she tried to pull back, to put some distance between them, but his arm was unyielding and with a small sigh of surrender, she gave herself up to the moment. The world was an unfeeling machine. She would not deny that. But for these few intoxicating moments she wouldn't think about it. She was trying to understand these guests. To do that, wouldn't it be useful to experience some of their feelings?

The waltz ended finally, and it was with regret that she made ready to follow him back to the table. But he didn't move; merely waited patiently for the music to begin again. This time it was an Old English court dance, and though she feared the figures were too intricate, she managed to follow him through it without any major errors.

They spent the rest of the evening on the dance floor. The orchestra played every conceivable kind of music, from disco and rock and roll, to waltz and square dance, and even some hauntingly dissonant music to which the dancers improvised their own steps.

By that time, the music and the atmosphere had worked their enchantment and Amber swayed and whirled with the rest, lost in her own sense of the strange music.

She applauded the selection of the knight and his lady dragon as winners of the prize for best costumes; though, as she confided to Kerr, she thought the huge spiders very original, if somewhat ugly.

And then the orchestra played the last waltz and she was abruptly aware that the evening was over. Back to reality, she told herself sharply as she watched the couples leave the ballroom together. She moistened her lips, and suddenly conscious of her hand still in Kerr's, carefully removed it.

"Thank you very much for the evening, Mr. Corrigan," she said with an attempt at a businesslike tone.

His eyes sparkled wickedly. "You're quite welcome, Mrs. Sinclair. As you can see, your concern about weapons was unnecessary."

With a start she realized that she hadn't given a thought to weapons since Zonan—Kerr, she corrected herself—had put his hand on his sword early in the evening. "Yes, yes," she stammered. "I can see that the weapons are no problem. At least, they weren't tonight. Well, thank you again. I'll be going now." She took a step toward the door.

"Wait." His voice was soft, but it stopped her even more swiftly than the hand he reached out to her arm. "I'll take you home."

"Oh, that won't be necessary. I live right here. Good night, Mr. Corrigan."

"Elizabeth-my-love . . ."

She couldn't help it. The words kept her from moving and she couldn't bring herself to shake off the strong, warm fingers that closed around her elbow. "I'm afraid that in this case your reality will have to concede to mine. I'm going to your door with you, whether you like it or not. Zonan doesn't let his companion wander alone through dangerous Viking territory."

His reference to Holden silenced her last objection. Though she'd been careful to put the man in a part of the hotel far from her suite, he might see her in the hall and follow her. "All right, Mr. Corrigan."

His only reaction to her repeated use of his last name was a slight tightening of his fingers as they slid down to take hers.

They were silent as they made their way through the

halls. The crowd thinned the farther they got from the ballroom, but when she tried to withdraw her fingers from his, he smiled and shook his head. "Remember the Vikings."

With a silent sigh, she let her hand remain where it was.

It was almost a shock to be back in the mundane atmosphere of the hotel halls. For a while there, the ballroom and Zonan-Kerr had seemed her whole universe. She bit her bottom lip. Thinking like that would only get her in trouble. That was the fallacy of trying to escape reality. You always had to come back to it in the end. And the contrast made the real world appear even more miserable.

She stopped at her door, only then remembering that the key lay in the warm valley between her breasts. "I . . . Excuse me." She turned away, but even so she couldn't prevent him from seeing what she was doing.

He was grinning as she turned back, key in hand. "An excellent hiding place," he said. "Secure from all but the most despicable villains. But too traditional. I thought you had more imagination than that."

"I have no imagination," she declared, wondering if he could understand how futilely she had tried to kill that dreaming, juvenile part of herself.

"I seem to be disagreeing with you all the time," he said cheerfully. "Our realities just don't connect. Yet. In mine, Elizabeth-my-love, you have a wonderful imagination. More than once it has come up with the way out of very dangerous places, for both of us. And in matters of love . . . There you are unsurpassable."

The intensity of his words made her head swim. "I . . . You . . ." She could think of nothing to say, nothing to do, to stem the terrible tide of longing that was rising in her.

"Thank you, Elizabeth-my-love, for an enchanted evening," he went on. "I've never had one so good, so beautiful . . ."

His eyes were on hers and she wondered desperately if he could read her thoughts there, thoughts that were both exciting and frightening. He must have read something, or maybe he just followed the impulses of his own reality. Anyway, he reached for her. His hands on her arms drew her into his embrace and a shiver of desire trembled down her spine. One part of her mind was clamoring about danger, but the rest of her didn't care. She wanted him to kiss her: she knew that with sudden clarity. She wanted one more touch of enchantment before she stopped being his Elizabeth.

Without conscious thought she lifted her mouth to his. His lips were warm on hers; soft, tender, persuasive. There was no invasion implied, no sense of mastery in his kiss. It was at the same time welcome and farewell, speaking eloquently of long acquaintance, of shared dangers, of shared joy.

When he released her, she could only stand there weakly, her head against his shoulder.

His lips were warm on her ear. "There's a very good speaker. Tomorrow at two. I think you'd be interested in what she has to say."

Still shaken by his kiss, she only vaguely heard his words. His hand went under her chin and he raised her face till her eyes met his. "I guess I have to leave you now."

His eyes were asking for an invitation, but she knew she dared not give it. "Yes," she stammered. "Th— thank you."

His arms fell away from her and she saw disappointment tighten his mouth. "Will I see you tomorrow?" he asked. "Will you come to hear the speaker?"

"I . . . don't know. Good night, Kerr." She turned to fumble with her key and so didn't catch his slight smile at her use of his first name again.

"Good night, Elizabeth-my-love. Sleep well."

She didn't trust herself to turn and look after him. She might call out the words clamoring in her mind. She might cry out, *Kerr, Kerr, don't go. Stay with me.*

The key finally found the lock and she turned it sharply. She slipped inside and closed the door quickly behind her. Standing there, her back pressed to it, she felt her heart pounding in her throat. She was being ridiculous. Kerr wouldn't try to follow her in. Not as himself or as Zonan.

She latched the door and went to stand in front of the mirror. The masked woman who stared back at her with sparkling eyes and heaving breasts was a stranger. With a sob, she ripped off the mask and turned away. It was not "good night"; it was "good-bye" to Elizabeth-my-love.

5

When she woke the next morning with the beginning of a headache, Amber felt the rightness of it. She had gone too far the night before, behaving like a child, forgetting the hard lesson Andy had taught her. A lump rose in her throat. For a while there she had almost believed Kerr, almost been taken in by his talk of a "different reality."

But the world was still the same place. Last night hadn't changed that, only made it harder to bear. Why hadn't she listened to her own words? The figure of the flying horse promised a world that couldn't be, an illusion that could only bring more unhappiness. Better not to dream. Better to remember the world as it was.

She forced herself out of the bed and into the shower, forced herself to perform the mechanical tasks of dressing and grooming, forced herself to go down to the office, all the while fighting hard, and not very successfully, to forget the magic of being Elizabeth, his Elizabeth.

Betsy was there early, her young face alive with curiosity. "Good morning, Mrs. Sinclair."

"Good morning, Betsy." To her own surprise Amber's voice sounded cheerful. "How are you this morning?" The question was routine, of course. Usually Betsy answered with a smiling "Fine." But this morning it was different.

"I'm just bubbling over with curiosity, Mrs. Sinclair. What kind of costume did Mr. Corrigan send you? What was the ball like? I know you had fun. Your eyes are sparkling."

Amber shook her head. Betsy was young and foolish. There was no point in getting angry with her. Nor in cutting her off with a sharp retort. Maybe this was the time for a little object lesson.

"The costume was like his." Amber tried to say this nonchalantly, but she couldn't help noticing the girl's eyes widen. Evidently Betsy saw the implications in that, too. Amber went on. "The ball was very interesting. I think I learned quite a bit about the way those people think."

Betsy's sudden giggle surprised her and made Amber ask "What's so funny?" in a tone that approached sharpness. She was trying to put this whole situation in the proper perspective and she didn't see any humor in it.

"I'm sorry, Mrs. Sinclair. It's just . . ." Betsy looked a trifle embarrassed. "Well, it's the way you said

69

'those people,' like . . . like they really *were* aliens or something.''

Somewhat shocked, Amber considered this observation and recognized its truth. She did consider these conventioneers almost a species apart. "I suppose I do think of them that way," she conceded. "I can't see why people don't just face up to reality."

Betsy looked as if she were about to say something, then thought better of it. "I suppose life looks different to different kinds of people," she said. "And anyway, I guess they don't think we're so great, either."

"What do you mean?" Amber battled a sense of annoyance. She wanted to forget the experience of last night, especially the experience of being in Kerr's arms, of feeling his kiss.

Betsy's giggle was irrepressible. "They call us mundane," she said. "Isn't that funny?"

Amber considered the word. It wasn't an insulting word. And it was more or less accurate. She shrugged. "Sounds like an adequate word to me. I wish the world would just be mundane all the time. I wouldn't ask for more."

Betsy's blonde eyebrows peaked as she frowned. "But there's no excitement in that. I read the other day that people need a certain amount of excitement in their lives."

Amber managed a smile, though this discussion was making her increasingly uncomfortable. "I think," she said, with a glance at Betsy's desk, "that if we don't want the excitement of looking for a new job, we'd better get to work."

Betsy didn't look properly chastened, but she nodded. "Yes, Mrs. Sinclair," she said and turned to her work.

Amber entered her office and sank down in her chair. The best way to forget last night was to concentrate on her work.

Two hours later she faced an empty desk. Why, she asked herself in exasperation, did she have to have a lull in her work right now? Why couldn't this be one of those harried, scrambling days when she hardly had time to think at all?

She had no answers to these questions, of course. Things in this world were not arranged to the liking of its inhabitants. Wishing that they were was only a childish weakness.

A quick glance at her watch told her that the first convention speaker would begin in ten minutes. She had no idea of going to hear her, of course. What those people said didn't make any sense.

She leaned back in her chair and closed her eyes. Immediately Kerr's face appeared in her mind. The dark tousled hair, the almost black eyes gleaming behind his scarf-mask, his bold nose and outthrust bearded chin. And then she savored the feel of his lips on hers, his body against hers, and she leapt to her feet.

She couldn't go on like this. She needed something, anything, to occupy her mind. Surely it wouldn't hurt to go hear this speaker. She knew these people were wrong. She knew the dangers of trying to make one's own little world. Living with Andy had taught her that.

Yes, that was the thing to do. Listening to this

speaker would give her more insight into the ways of these guests. And if she happened to see Kerr there, well, she had to make arrangements to return the costume to him, the costume she had so neatly folded before coming to work this morning.

She pushed back her chair and rose, glancing in the mirror at her hair. Betsy was right, she realized, her eyes were sparkling and her color was high. But it was because she was upset by this intrusion into her life, not because she was excited. Though she had to admit that the beginnings of her headache were completely gone.

She stepped out into the outer office. "I'll be out for an hour or so," she told Betsy. "If there's an emergency, I'll be in Room 210. For a while, at least."

"Yes, Mrs. Sinclair."

The look on the young secretary's face caused Amber to add, "I want to learn more about this kind of guest."

"Yes, Mrs. Sinclair." Amber was already out the door by then, so she didn't see Betsy's knowing smile or hear her whisper to herself, "I'd bet a week's pay that *he'll* be there."

Amber chose a seat near the middle of the room. Just as she sank into it a diminutive woman stepped up behind the podium. Amber assessed her quickly. Outside of this room, she would never have recognized this woman as a conventioneer. Her silver hair was beautifully coiffed and she wore a soft feminine suit and matching pumps. At least sixty, Amber thought, and she has money. Lots of it. The understated clothes testified to that. And to class.

With an effort Amber kept herself from looking around the room for Kerr. Her eyes had swept it automatically on her way in and she hadn't seen him then, but he could have entered behind her. Forget about him, she told herself. Concentrate on what this woman is saying. Look for the fallacies. It will keep your mind occupied.

The speaker looked out over the assembled listeners and smiled. "Good morning. I've been asked to speak to you today about the worlds of science fiction. Let me say before I begin that I'd far rather this be a discussion than a lecture. So if you have something to say, feel free to say it."

A shiver ran down Amber's spine and she knew suddenly, inexplicably, that *he* was in the room. Her hands tightened in her lap as she strove not to turn and look for him. She could keep her head immobile, her eyes focused on the woman in the front of the room, but she couldn't keep her body from remembering the feel of his, her lips from recalling his kiss.

At first Amber had to force herself to pay attention to the speaker. But soon—very soon—she realized why Kerr had suggested *this* speaker. The ideas being advanced were very like his. They were beautiful ideas, she had to grant that.

Imagine a world where you could be in another person's mind and experience his joys and sorrows as you would your own. And where he could do the same. Imagine love in a world like that. Imagine knowing, really knowing, another person like that. How could you hurt someone, she wondered, if you had to experience that hurt yourself? How could you keep someone from doing what he wanted and needed to do, if you were feeling his need with him?

For a moment she let her thoughts carry her along these lines. How wonderful to live in a world like that. How wonderful never to be alone again.

And then her mind replied harshly: Don't be a fool. Such a world doesn't exist. It never has. It never will.

Sudden tears rose to her eyes and she swallowed hastily. That was the trouble with all beautiful things, things of the imagination. They were all illusion. To become attached to them was to invite disaster.

She raised her hand.

"Yes?"

"All this is very nice," she said and she knew that Kerr was listening. "But this kind of literature is essentially useless. The worlds you've been talking about are only imagined. They don't exist. They never will. They only make people even more dissatisfied with the world that is."

The woman at the podium smiled gently. "That's what people used to say about other things that were considered impossible. About space flight. About going to the moon. Even about such mundane things as the telephone and television. All that it took to make these 'impossible things' real was someone's belief in their possibility, someone's commitment to making the imagined into the real."

"But those are 'things,'" Amber blurted out. "Things can be made, designed. People are different."

"People *are* different," the speaker conceded. "But the principle is the same. What I'm trying to say in my books, what many writers are trying to say, is that belief can make things happen. They're saying now that every thought ever thought is still in existence. Maybe if enough of us think that things like telepathy and total empathy are possible, they'll become so. Belief is what makes our reality, after all."

Amber could find no words of rebuttal. The whole idea was clearly foolish. You couldn't change the world by believing it different any more than you could fix a flat tire by wishing it fixed. Childish dreams, that's what these people had. Childish dreams that were not only foolish but destructive. What happened to the poor person whose belief was never justified; the person who was forced finally to confront the real world?

She had been such a person once, living in that marvelous sunny world of Andy's—that world where everything was bright and beautiful. And then she'd been forced to face reality, to realize that that whole sunny world was unreal—a sham. The tears rose to her eyes and she blinked rapidly. She was never going to be hurt like that again. Never. Because now she knew better. Now she knew that her parents had been right. She asked for no more golden dreams; she knew them for the deception they were.

The buzz of voices around her brought Amber to the realization that the speaker had left the podium. She swallowed over the lump in her throat and got to her feet. This place was not where she should be. She moved down the aisle toward the door and then she saw him. He was clear across the room, but she knew his eyes were on her. She jerked her gaze away and hurried out, back to her office. She couldn't speak to him. Not now.

An hour later Amber got up from her desk and began to pace the floor. She couldn't sit still for another minute. This convention was driving her crazy. All these strange ideas. And the people . . .

Why should she be feeling disappointed that Kerr hadn't followed her back to her office? Hadn't she hurried out of the room so she wouldn't have to talk to him? She frowned and pulled at the hem of her brown jacket. This couldn't go on. This terrible restlessness. This need to . . . She stopped that thought. Enough. She was going out to walk the corridors. That was acceptable behavior in a hotel manager. And maybe she could burn off some of this nervous energy that wouldn't let her be.

She'd made a complete circuit of the third floor, satisfied that everything was in order there, and was halfway around the second when she turned a corner and almost ran into Everett Holden. His costume had been replaced by slacks and a shirt, but his eyes were still the rapacious, greedy ones of a Viking raider.

"Why, hello there, Mrs. Sinclair. You're looking real pretty this morning."

"Good morning, Mr. Holden." She had to work hard to inject any cordiality into her words. There was something about the man that rubbed her the wrong way. She couldn't wait to get away from him. She moved to the right, but Holden moved, too. Keeping her face serene, she moved to the left. So did he.

"Don't go yet, honey."

How she hated to be called pet names by strangers. It was so demeaning. And having this man do it infuriated her. "I have work to do, Mr. Holden." She tried to keep her voice even, not to let him hear how much she disliked this game he was playing. He was, after all, a guest here. Remember that, she told herself silently.

"Come on," he said, sliding closer. "Old Ev just wants to be friends."

Amber became aware that once again the man had been helping himself rather bountifully to the free beer. "You live around here?" he asked.

She didn't dignify that with an answer. "I have to get back to my office," she said.

"It *was* you I saw last night," Holden cried suddenly. "That Corrigan has the nerve! Telling me you're engaged to him!"

"I don't know what you're talking about," Amber said, hoping she could keep her face from giving her away.

"Yes, you do, honey." Holden was determined now. "He thought he had me fooled, but it was you, all right. I recognize that mole on your cheek. Elizabeth, indeed! Yeah, it was you. Listen . . ."

He took a step closer and she moved backward. Unfortunately that put her back against the corridor wall.

"Why don't you and me go out tonight?" Holden

suggested. "We could paint the town. A chick like you oughtta know all the best places."

Amber swallowed over the lump in her throat. Her stomach was beginning to churn from the smell of stale beer and from fright. No, she wasn't exactly afraid of him. But she didn't want to make a scene in her own hotel.

"Mr. Holden, the hotel frowns on its employees fraternizing with guests." For a moment she thought he would believe her. Then he scowled. "You went out with him, with that glorified—"

"Good morning, Mrs. Sinclair. Holden. Isn't it a great morning?"

Amber's sense of relief was so strong she could have thrown herself into Kerr's arms as he came from around the corner. In the black slacks and shirt he was wearing that day he didn't look as dashing as his make-believe character, but his rescue was every bit as effective as it would have been had he come on horseback, flourishing a sword.

"Hello, Mr. Corrigan." She appreciated his thoughtfulness in addressing her formally and responded in kind.

Holden turned to meet the newcomer and Amber took the opportunity to move into the center of the corridor, nearer to Kerr.

"'Morning." Holden's greeting was almost sullen.

Kerr didn't seem to notice. He turned his pleasant smile on Amber. "I was just coming to ask you. I forgot what time I'm picking you up for dinner."

Amber's mouth fell open with surprise, but fortunately Holden had turned to look at Kerr. She recovered quickly. "Oh, about seven sounds good." She hoped Kerr would get the point as she continued. "Will you have a list of those items we mean to discuss about next year's convention?"

Kerr's face was serious, but his eyes twinkled at her. "Of course." He sent Holden a friendly glance and commented cheerfully, "Mrs. Sinclair has kindly consented to have dinner with me. We're going to get everything set for next year."

He clapped the other man heartily on the back and for a moment Amber thought Holden might explode. He certainly looked like a candidate for a heart attack. Thank goodness she didn't often run into men like him.

"Have a good day, Mr. Holden," she said before turning to the man at her side. "Mr. Corrigan? If you're not busy, perhaps you'd walk along with me. There's something I want to show you." And leaving a fuming Holden behind them they strolled off.

Amber waited until they were around the corner and halfway down the next corridor before she slowed her pace. "Thank you, Mr. Corrigan. I couldn't seem—"

"Hey, none of that Mister stuff. Today the name is Kerr."

His smile warmed her whole body, but she didn't want to think about that. "All right, thank you, Kerr. I couldn't seem to put him off." She managed a little smile. "He knows I am—was—Elizabeth. Or at least he suspects so. He noticed the mole on my cheek."

Kerr nodded. "Just stay firm if he bothers you again. I happen to know he's been offered a job in Chicago, so he won't be around after the convention is over."

Amber breathed a sigh of relief. "That's good." She turned to move off. "Well, thanks again. I'll be getting back to my office."

Kerr nodded. "See you at seven."

That stopped her again. "Oh, no!" She paused, flustered. "I mean, you don't need to really take me to dinner. I appreciate your help, but . . ."

His grin was slightly wicked. "I thought maybe we'd go to the Pier. Their seafood is excellent."

Amber shook her head. "No, I can't. You know the hotel's policy . . ."

He chuckled. "We'll talk business. For a while."

His eyes met hers and the blood rushed to her face. "Mr. Corrigan. Kerr . . . I . . . You helped me with Mr. Holden, but . . ."

"Come on," he said. "I was going to ask you to dinner anyway. Holden just made it easier." His look turned serious. "Come on, I did you a favor. Now you can do me one."

His logic didn't make any sense and she knew it, but she suddenly wanted very much to say yes. "Well, if you're sure."

"I'm positive," he said. "There's just one thing."

"Yes?" Her reply was automatic. She was already mentally reviewing the contents of her closet.

"Well, two things actually. Please let your hair hang free, and don't wear one of those business suits. Let me see you in something soft and feminine. Okay?"

He didn't wait for her answer. "See you later, Elizabeth-my-love."

And he was gone so quickly that she couldn't bring any words up past her suddenly immobile tongue. She hurried off in the opposite direction, trying hard to escape the echo of those words in her head. "Elizabeth-my-love. Elizabeth-my-love."

6

~eeeeeeeeee~

At ten minutes before seven Amber was pacing the narrow confines of her living room. The lime green dress with its crisscrossed bodice and filmy floating skirt felt odd after so many days of business suits. So did having her hair down. She adjusted the wristband on one long full sleeve and turned, retracing her steps.

She was being foolish, of course. But what harm could it do to comply with such innocent requests? Long hair was unsuitable for the office. And so was this dress—a dress that she had bought one year, in a gesture of defiance, for a Christmas party and had not worn since. It was a lovely dress; it made her feel fragile and delicate. And very, very feminine. So did the bronze sandals, with their high heels and whisper-thin straps.

Yes, there was no doubt that these clothes made her look—and feel—very different from her usual everyday self. But surely dinner with a man called for something a little special. Especially this man.

She had reached the window again in her pacing and paused to look out at the wide expanse of the Mississippi River. The setting sun had gilded its waves, transforming the view into a real-life painting. Around the lawn below, the flower beds were alive with the beauty of blooming May flowers. More illusion, she reminded herself sharply. The flowers lasted hardly any longer than the golden sunlight on the river. She turned away, spinning on her heel. She was going to put her hair up, whether he liked it that way or not. After all . . .

A sharp rap on the door stopped her in midstride and she almost twisted her ankle as she turned swiftly in the flimsy sandal. "Coming!"

She crossed the room and pulled open the door. For a moment they stared at each other. She was not at all sure she could do more than that. Just looking at him took her breath away. He spoke finally, softly. "I was wrong last night. You're the most beautiful woman, not just in Memphis, but in the whole world. That dress makes you look like a goddess."

"Thank you," she managed to stammer. "You . . . you look pretty good yourself." His tan suit set off his dark good looks and his beard and mustache combined with those burning black eyes to give him a slightly dangerous look. She felt her heart pounding in her throat, the blood racing through her veins.

"Thank you," he returned. His eyes traveled over her, appreciative masculine eyes. She felt her color rising, felt her body becoming more and more conscious of his.

"Well," he said, "shall we go let the world see what a stunning pair we are?"

"Yes." It was all she could do to get the word out. How could any one man have such an effect on her?

The Pier was a big old wooden building. Once a warehouse and icehouse for fishing boats, it fronted the Mississippi, some distance farther toward the downtown section of the city than the hotel. As they got out of the car, Kerr pulled her hand through his arm. "Have you ever been for a ride on a paddlewheel steamer?" he asked, gesturing with his other arm toward the river and the several paddle wheels anchored along the shore.

Amber shook her head. "No. I . . . I haven't had time."

He looked as if he were about to say something to this, to reprimand her for neglecting one of Memphis's most interesting experiences. "I don't suppose you've been to Mud Island, either," he said finally, exasperation in his voice. "Or to Beale Street."

"I did the walking tour of Beale Street when I first came here," she replied, glad she could say something to convince him that she wasn't a complete ignoramus where the city was concerned.

"And when was that?"

"Oh, about a year ago."

"They've done a lot more since then," he said. "The renovation of Beale Street is something to see. I especially like the old theaters. Places like that ought to be preserved."

She did not see why he should get sentimental over some old buildings, but she did not say so. For some reason she didn't want to emphasize the differences between them tonight. Her hand through his arm, her body conscious of his nearness, she gazed out over the river. The sun was lower in the sky now, casting its golden glow over the red and white paddle wheels. She had to admit that a ride on one of them sounded like fun. "Maybe in a few weeks," she said, "I'll have some more time. Then I'll take another tour of the city."

His grin was devilish. "See that you do that," he said. "Imagine living in Memphis and never having done those things." He shook his head. "You've been living a deprived life, Amber Sinclair."

She was perfectly willing to agree with that, though she didn't think the worst deprivation was being unaware of the points of interest of the city in which she lived and worked. She didn't intend to tell him that, though. Let him think what he liked about her. She knew that it had taken all her energy to get through those first days and nights at the hotel, to prove herself in this new position of responsibility. And, she admitted to herself silently, to recover from the pain of her parting with Andy, of the final loss of the dream she'd been nourishing, unaware, through all those terrible years of marriage.

A warm spring breeze crossed the river and cooled her cheeks as Kerr turned her back toward the restaurant. "This place used to be an icehouse," he explained, his hand on her elbow. "There's a lot of the original equipment left. Motors and such. You'll see inside."

Amber nodded as he moved her off, up the weathered wooden stairs. She did try to take in the atmosphere of the place, but all she really retained was the impression of lots of old wood, high ceilings, and great thick ropes. All her senses were tuned to Kerr. His every glance, his every move, his every word, seemed vitally important to her. Memphis or Timbuktu, it was all the same to her.

He pulled her chair out, his fingers brushing for one fleeting instance across the bare flesh of her back and making her body fire with a wish that she could step once more into his arms.

Instead she straightened and watched him seat himself. Her eyes couldn't seem to get enough of him, she thought with a sense of dismay. What ever had happened to the sane, sensible Amber that she usually was?

"I can recommend the catfish and steak special," he said softly. "But order whatever appeals to you."

"That sounds fine." She flushed. She hadn't even bothered to open the menu that lay before her. She tried to pull herself together, to appear as a sensible businesswoman. "You said," she began, her tongue suddenly thick, "that is . . . this is a business dinner."

Kerr's chuckle was warm, and the look in his eyes

was anything but businesslike. "Come on now, Amber. That was strictly for Holden's benefit and you know it."

"Well, but . . ." She didn't know how to go on.

He sighed dramatically. "Here I went to all the trouble to get you alone—away from that cell you call an office, and look how you're behaving."

She felt only a touch of pique, but she made an effort to defend herself. "It's not a cell. I'm a businesswoman, you know. Not a female adventurer."

His eyes made her blood race and her flesh tingle. "That's your reality," he said softly. "In mine . . ." He paused and his eyes moved over her briefly, but not so briefly that her body didn't respond to their perusal. Part of her mind cautioned her that he was dangerous, this man who could make her feel so different, who could erase all the lessons she had learned so painfully from her marriage to Andy.

But another part kept reminding her that Andy was only *one* man. Most of all, this rebellious part of her mind kept insisting on one thing—she wanted Kerr Corrigan.

She was no longer a child, but a mature woman. And that woman wanted Kerr; she wanted him very badly. That didn't mean, however, that she was going to do anything about it, she told herself with a sense of desperation, except to have this dinner with him.

"In *my* reality you are a female adventurer. The best. My friend, my companion." His voice dropped an octave. "My lover."

It was the second time he had called her that. The

blood rushed to her face, raced through her veins, pounded in her heart. "I . . ." she began, but she was unable to go on.

"How long have you been in the hotel business?" he asked, changing his tone.

Gratefully she stopped to collect her thoughts. "Seven years."

"Do you like it?"

Did she like it? She tried to think. It was not a question she had ever considered. "I . . . never thought about it. I guess I do. It's a job."

"Just a job."

She knew from his voice that he didn't like her answer. "What's wrong with that?"

He shrugged. "Nothing, I suppose. I just thought a woman like you . . ." His voice made the word a caress. "I thought you would want a job with challenge. Something that was fun."

Amber stiffened slightly. "A woman like me," she replied rather crisply, "needs first a job to support herself. Food and shelter come before self-fulfillment, you know."

"I know." His voice was conciliatory. "But you have so much potential."

"I do enjoy my job," she continued, warming to her subject. "And as for challenge . . ." Her eyes sought his. "There's more than one Holden in the world, you know."

His shoulders slumped dramatically and his face grew downcast. "And here I thought *I* was your challenge."

For a moment she couldn't reply—her tongue

seemed to have become unmanageable—then she finally stammered, "We were talking about my job."

He nodded gravely, but the twinkle was still there in his eyes. "So we were."

"It isn't easy to manage a big hotel," Amber went on, trying to keep her mind on business and knowing that that wouldn't be easy, either, not with this man sitting across from her. "There are conventions." She smiled at him with mischief in her eyes. "Some strange people come to conventions, you know. Some very strange people."

His laugh rang out through the quiet restaurant. "People like us," he said, his voice vibrating with humor. "Those strange birds who like science fiction."

She nodded, matching her mood to his. "That's right. People who run around in costumes." She shook her head. "And carrying weapons, yet. Of course," she added, her smile growing, "to be absolutely fair, I must admit that we get other guests who are troublesome. Alumni who gather to cheer on their old alma mater and who are somewhat the worse for too much beer, hosiery salesmen gathered to learn new techniques, and not necessarily for selling hose."

Kerr grinned. "Go on," he said. "It sounds fascinating, really fascinating."

"Well, there are little old ladies with Great Danes, newlyweds who aren't speaking to each other, kids who play cowboys and Indians in the hall." She shrugged. "We get all kinds. And then, there are things like broken pipes and air-conditioning units that won't work and people who think their sheets aren't clean." She smiled. "I could go on and on."

Kerr's smile was warm, but the hand that covered hers was warmer, and it was raising the temperature of her body. "Yes, I suppose you could," he said.

The waitress arrived then. Amber flushed as she withdrew her fingers from Kerr's. When the waitress had gone with their orders, Kerr asked, "What are you doing in Memphis? It's clear you're not from here originally."

"I thought I needed to be on my own," she replied. "My parents . . ." She paused, wondering briefly why she was opening herself to this stranger. "My parents teach science. It's their whole life. They disapproved of my marriage." She flushed. "They said it was just a bad case of hormones."

Kerr didn't laugh. "Nothing wrong with hormones," he said.

She shrugged again. "My parents thought so. They don't have time for anything but science. They told me I was making a mistake, that I should look for a sensible man. But I wanted to have fun." The word sounded like a curse, the curse it had been for her.

"Nothing wrong with fun, either," he said gently.

"Maybe not. But it's certainly not the only thing in life. Except for people like Andy."

"Andy was your husband." His quiet statement encouraged her to go on.

"Yes. When I met him . . ." She shook her head. "I suppose I was some kind of classic case. My parents had no time for fun. Like I said, they're scientists. For them the universe is a big machine rolling relentlessly on. Your best chance of survival is figuring out how the elements in it work. And keeping out of the way."

Kerr nodded. "The old school of thought."

Momentarily she wondered what he meant by that, but she was caught up in telling her story and didn't stop to ask.

"He was a butterfly, Andy was. New places fascinated him. They were fun, he said. And drinking and partying were fun." She swallowed over the lump in her throat. "If it wasn't fun, Andy didn't do it."

Kerr's tone was gentle. "What *didn't* he do?"

Her laughter was brittle; she didn't like the sound of it. She didn't know why she was telling Kerr all this. But for the life of her, she couldn't stop. "For one thing, he didn't pay the bills. Or, maybe I should just say, he didn't work."

She lingered, remembering. "When I first met him, I thought he was the most wonderful man in the world. Warm. Alive. Exciting. My parents were awfully stuffy. Andy swept me up into a wonderful new world."

She sighed. "I was too young and stupid to see that it was a false world, built of lies, on lies. Not one solid, dependable thing in it. Especially not Andy."

"Did he leave you?" Kerr asked softly.

Amber nodded her head. "More or less. One day when I came home, he was getting ready to move on. And I just couldn't do it. My job was the only good thing in my life. I couldn't give it up. I asked him to stay with me or go on without me."

"So he moved on without you."

"Yes. That was over a year ago. I got a chance at a promotion and came south for a while."

"Weren't you lonely away from your parents?" he asked. "I'd imagine they were happy to see you leave a man like that." He recaptured her hand and held it between his two warm ones. For some reason she was unable to marshal the strength to pull it away.

She smiled sadly. "Oh, they were. Very happy. But I couldn't handle their I-told-you-so expressions. I know I made a mistake. I don't need constant reminders."

"They don't sound like bad people," Kerr said rather absently.

Amber glanced at him with surprise. "I never said they were. They're just sure they have 'the facts' about everything." She heard her voice rising and couldn't stop it. "Sometimes I hate science!" Appalled, she shut her mouth with a snap. What ever had made her say a foolish thing like that?

But Kerr didn't seem to think it foolish. He nodded and stared at her solemnly, patting her captive hand. "You mean because it seems to have killed imagination."

She found herself nodding. This was crazy, her mind said. There was no such 'thing" as imagination, or beauty, or any of those other illusions foolish people pursued.

"But all science isn't like that," Kerr went on, his hand still around hers. "Some sciences rely heavily on the imagination."

She forced herself to concentrate on his words and not on what his touch was doing to her body. "Not according to my parents."

He shrugged his shoulders. "There was Einstein. He was certainly imaginative. And quantum physicists use their imaginations all the time."

Amber stared at him. "Quantum physicists?" she repeated. "What do you know about them?"

He looked a little amused and also a little sheepish. "I'm afraid I *am* one."

She couldn't believe her ears. "You! A scientist! I . . ." The laughter hit her then. A scientist! Her parents would never believe this. "You're putting me on," she said finally. "I can't believe a physicist would run around in that costume. Would waste a whole weekend at some silly thing like this convention."

His expression grew severe. "Regardless of what your parents taught you, Amber, the imagination is a very important scientific tool. I come to these conventions, just as I read science fiction literature, to give my imagination exercise. To encourage it to grow. Many great scientific discoveries are the product of imagination."

She wanted to believe him. She wanted desperately to believe him. What if that part of herself that was drawn to beauty and adventure, that part that had responded so happily to being Kerr's Elizabeth-my-love, was really a useful part? What if it had some practical application? The possibilities unfolded before her in shimmering glory. The biggest and brightest of them all, the chance of a real, lasting relationship with Kerr Corrigan.

"Excuse me." The waitress's muttered comment brought Amber back to reality and as Kerr released her hand, she looked down at her dinner. Some sane part of her mind, admittedly very small at the moment, told her she was being foolish again, asking to be hurt, hurt as Andy had hurt her. But another part insisted otherwise. What Kerr said made sense, a lot of sense. And the fact that she wanted it to make sense was really immaterial. If facts were facts, as her parents had insisted, then what she wanted or didn't want was ultimately not important at all. And cheered by this bit of convoluted theory, she dismissed the subject for the moment and picked up her fork.

7

Amber relaxed against the seat of the car as the LTD purred along. "Thank you for the dinner," she said softly. "It was very good. The best catfish I've ever had."

His eyes met hers for a moment before they returned to the road. "It's the best I've ever had, too. I think it was because of the company."

She flushed in the car's darkness, glad that he couldn't see her reaction. His compliments made her uncomfortable, perhaps because they reminded her of Andy's winning way with words. And the emptiness hidden behind his charming phrases. "Why do you read science fiction?" she asked. She would rather hear about him than listen to compliments.

"Why do I read science fiction?" he repeated thoughtfully. "I guess I like the freedom it gives me.

Like your Pegasus—to fly beyond myself. To experience new realities."

"But that's just the thing," she said plaintively. "None of those realities exist. They're just make-believe, illusion." She was aware now that she wanted him to refute this, to tell her it wasn't so.

He shrugged. "Eastern philosophers will tell you that everything is illusion, life itself is illusion. They want people to let go, to detach themselves from everything."

Amber frowned. "I don't understand that. Everyone has to have something to hang on to, to work for . . ." She paused, remembering Andy. "At least to *want*. Otherwise there's no point in living. We might as well all commit suicide."

"My feelings exactly," Kerr replied and she wondered why his voice carried that undertone of triumph. "So," he continued. "If life's all an illusion we might as well pick the one we like best. Right?"

"Well . . ." she hesitated. "I suppose so, *if* that's true. But I don't believe it. Life is real, all right. It goes right on, no matter what we do. Or believe. What's the point of trying to forget that, of living illusory lives in imaginary worlds? Sooner or later a person has to come back to this world, to the cold harsh reality of it."

Convince me, she pleaded silently. *Make me believe.*

"I guess life's been hard on you," he said quietly. "I'm sorry about that. But you have to take control." His voice grew determined. "Your life belongs to *you*. You can do what you want to with it."

Her laugh was brittle. "Tell me another fairy tale."

"I mean it, Amber."

Hearing him say her first name was almost as unsettling as having him call her Elizabeth-my-love.

"You can take charge of your life," he went on.

"Sure, sure." She couldn't keep the sarcasm out of her voice. "Tomorrow I can become the prima ballerina of the New York City Ballet."

He shook his head. "No, of course you can't. But if you wanted to, wanted it with all your heart and soul, and if you were willing to work for it, some day you might."

Amber frowned. "I can't believe that. I wanted my marriage to last." She hadn't meant to bring Andy into this again, but she couldn't help it. "I wanted it to be beautiful and good." Her voice was flat. "It didn't last. It was cheap and tawdry. Nothing I did could change that." She stared out the window at the passing houses, trying hard to control the rising tears.

She sighed deeply. She wished, really wished, that there were some way she could believe him. The world he was talking about would be much nicer to live in than the one she knew. But facts are facts, said her mother's voice in her head. And wishing doesn't change them. Hadn't she learned that the hard way?

"It isn't what happens to us that counts," Kerr said, as he turned into the hotel's parking lot. "It's how we feel about it that makes our reality."

He slipped into a parking space and turned off the key. For a moment there was silence in the car. The memory of his kiss the night before rose up to haunt her. She didn't want to think about that now, it was too . . .

Kerr got out and came around to open the door for her. Suddenly embarrassed, she tried to continue the conversation as she took the helping hand he extended. "I don't see how fooling yourself about reality can help anything."

He waited till she was erect, then pulled her arm through his. "It's not fooling," he said patiently. "Take tonight for instance. You know, you and I probably see tonight very differently."

"It was just a simple business dinner." She wished her voice wouldn't waver like that, like it always did when she tried to lie.

"For you, maybe. Not for me."

She knew she should keep silent, but she couldn't. "What do you mean?" she stammered.

"I think you know what I mean," he replied. And he was right. No one could mistake the look he was giving her then.

"Sh—shall we go sit by the pool?" she asked. "It's lovely this time of night."

For a moment she thought he would laugh at her, but he only replied, "If you like."

The inner courtyard that housed the pool was empty. He drew two chairs into a shadowed spot between some palms. "Is this okay?"

"Yes. Fine." She wondered briefly what she was doing here. She knew she didn't want to leave him yet. But that wasn't all of it. Her body kept reminding her of his kiss and of the sensations it had provoked in her.

"I guess I know why you don't read science fiction," he said, continuing their conversation. The shadows on his face made it even more dark and mysterious-looking. "Have you ever tried it?"

"No. I . . . I don't have much time for reading now. I'm concentrating on my career."

"So that's what you really want. To be a big career woman."

No! The voice in her head screamed so loudly that she thought he must have heard it. She bit her bottom lip. No, she didn't want a career. She wanted a husband and a home and children. That was the dream she had carried into her marriage with Andy. An unrealizable dream, she knew now. Oh, she might someday have them all—husband, home, and children. But it wouldn't be the same. There was no haze of glory around the images now. What was it Bacon had said? Something about loving people and thus giving hostages to fortune? If you loved, you got hurt. It was that simple.

She realized that Kerr was looking at her expectantly. "Yes." She managed the lie. The truth made her too vulnerable. "Yes, I have my career."

He was silent for a few minutes and her chair began to feel more and more uncomfortable. "You know," he said finally, "you remind me very much of one of Boris's covers."

"Boris?" His change of topic confused her.

"Boris Vallejo. I told you about him before. He does science fiction cover art."

Amber nodded. Now she remembered.

"Yes." Kerr frowned thoughtfully. "There's one of his paintings in particular. A warrior maiden."

She stiffened, thinking of the picture they had seen in the art gallery.

Kerr chuckled. "No, not like the glossy in the exhibit. Boris's women are real. Beautiful. This one has long red hair. And a beautiful body."

His voice had grown soft and caressing. Amber's body began to grow warm.

"She's riding a horse," he went on. "Yes, she looks just like you."

She tried to control her body's reactions. But her body wasn't listening. It was responding to the passion in his voice, to the soft tracery of his fingers in the open palm of her hand.

"In fact," he said, and there was a slight hint of laughter in his voice, "I happen to have a book with that very picture in it up in my room."

The silence grew heavy, the tension between them rising. "Would you like to see it?"

Yes! Again some part of her mind was quick to reply, but she remained silent, considering. There was far more to this than an offer to show her a picture. He was offering her something else, something she was aware that she wanted quite badly, so badly that her heart was pounding in her throat and her whole body was turning to fire. "I . . ."

"Please, Amber." His voice was a gentle caress, a quiet promise. "Please."

For some reason that quiet plea decided her. She tried to make her voice calm and businesslike; though why she did so she couldn't tell. Only a fool would mistake his intent. "Yes, I'd like to see your picture."

His eyes twinkled. "Shall we go up, then?"

She almost changed her mind a dozen times before they reached his door. But her body overcame all her mind's objections. This was a physical need she had, like eating and sleeping. And it had gone unsatisfied for a long time. But there was more to it than that, as she was well aware. There was a magic about Kerr that drew her to him. No matter that magic didn't exist, that she didn't believe in it. For tonight, everything was different.

Kerr unlocked his door and stood back for her to enter. Her body was trembling now. She didn't know whether it was from fear or excitement. He flicked the switch and light filled the room. Of course, she told herself, the picture. He really does have that picture.

He gestured toward the table and chairs. "Sit down. I'll be right there."

Crossing the room on trembling legs, she sank into a chair. She turned to watch him over her shoulder as he pulled open a drawer and took out several large art books. Laughter bubbled in her throat, surprising her. He evidently meant to show her more than one picture.

He put the books on the table in front of her and pulled the other chair up close to hers. Amber looked at the cover of the top book. A blonde warrior with hair to her waist and the absolute minimum of clothing stood posed with each hand resting on a repellent-looking dinosaurlike creature. Amber suppressed a shiver. "I think I prefer horses."

Kerr's chuckle was low and warm and she felt his

breath on her ear as he settled into the chair beside her. "Those are her pets," he said. "Primeval princesses have rather different tastes."

"I guess so." She heard her own voice with a sense of surprise. She could hardly believe that she was doing this. "She is beautiful," she said, directing her attention to the figure's face. "She looks strong and independent."

Kerr's voice was even. "She's a princess," he said, as though that explained everything. "But she's not the one I want you to see." He picked up one of the books and began to turn the pages. "Here she is."

Amber drew a sharp breath. This was no glossy surrealistic picture, half woman, half machine, such as they had seen in the exhibit. This woman was completely female. Yet there was nothing weak or vulnerable about her. In spite of the fact that her armbands, boots, and high-collared necklace covered more flesh than her golden loincloth and bra, her face wore a look of imperious command. She was carrying a drawn sword and riding a fine mettlesome horse. Yes, Amber thought, she looked ready for any situation. "She's beautiful," she whispered, forgetting for the moment the comparison he had made to herself.

His arm went around her shoulders and his lips touched her ear as he whispered, "She looks like you. Only you're more beautiful."

She shook her head. "Don't be silly. I don't look like that. Oh, her hair might be the same shade, but . . ."

"Well . . ." His voice carried an undertone of amusement. "I haven't seen you in a costume like that, but I bet you'd look every bit as good." He lifted her hand and kissed the palm. Desire shivered over her aching body and she closed her eyes, swaying toward him, her face turning automatically toward his.

His lips were warm and soft. Gentle and tender, they covered hers and with a muffled little cry she turned her body to meet his, completely forgetting the intervening arms of the chairs between them.

When he released her mouth, he kept his arm around her shoulders and drew her to her feet. She took the one step that separated them and was in his arms. The world with all its facts fell away. There was only this moment, this moment in the warm haven of his embrace.

He held her so for long moments, her body close to him, as his lips explored the mouth she turned up to his. She felt her body softening, yearning to mold with his, and she pressed herself against him.

One moment he was kissing her and the next he had scooped her easily into his arms and was carrying her to the wide bed. She did not protest, but clung to him, her arms around his neck, her cheek against his suit jacket.

He put her gently on the bed and his hands moved to the wisps of sandals. She felt his fingers against her instep as he carefully removed one. Oh, she wanted him. So much she wanted him.

He put the other sandal on the floor and smiled at her. "You're so beautiful," he said softly. "So very beautiful."

She wasn't, she knew. She might be reasonably attractive; she was not beautiful. But at the moment it didn't matter. At the moment she could believe him. She felt beautiful. Soft, and warm, and beautiful.

His hands spanned her slender waist; moved to untie the sash that was knotted there. Then he gathered her in one arm as he might a child, and with the fingers of his other hand he drew the long zipper of her dress downward. He pulled the dress down over her hips and put it on one of the chairs.

"You looked good in it," he said as he settled beside her. "But you look better in this."

She was glad she had worn one of her lacy bras. Not really an extravagance since they cost no more than the other kind. The blood raced to her face as his eyes devoured her. She hoped she looked as good as he had thought she would.

His hands covered her breasts and she felt her nipples rising against the silky material. He ran a finger up the curve of her throat to her softly parted lips before he bent to drop a quick kiss there. Then his hands moved under her, behind her back, and her bra came away. "Even more beautiful," he said, tossing it away. He hooked his fingers in the elastic at her waist, taking half-slip, panty hose, and panties down in one swift motion. And she lay naked before him.

For several minutes he just sat there, feasting his eyes on her, and she let herself relax, let herself bask in his admiration. Suddenly he bent and dropped a kiss on each erect nipple, then got to his feet. "Be right back," he said.

First he turned down the light, leaving the room in a soft glow. Then quickly, yet with a lithe grace, he

removed his clothes. She watched him with un-
abashed curiosity, allowing herself to realize to the full
how deeply his body had affected hers. It hadn't really
been his costume, though that had certainly attracted
her notice. It had been the man himself.

She admired the lean muscular planes of his bare
back as he bent to take off his shoes and socks, his
dark chest covered with fine black hair. His trousers
dropped to the floor and he stepped out of them. His
legs were well-muscled, too, and . . .

Too long, her body cried. Oh, it's been too long.

Then he was beside her, drawing her into his arms,
and body met body. She trembled from the contact, burrowing against him as though she could hide
there.

He lifted the screen of hair from her shoulder and
kissed it gently. "Such beautiful skin," he whispered,
his breath warm on her flesh. A little shiver trembled
over her and she buried her face in the curve between
his throat and shoulder. She could feel the long lean
length of his body against hers, feel the good contact
of flesh against flesh, skin against skin. Her body
seemed to be soaking up the feel of his, like land that
had suffered through a long drought and now felt the
welcoming touch of rain. She sighed, giving herself up
to the joy of touching and being touched.

His lips covered hers, more urgent now, and her
own responded. His hands moved across her back,
gently stroking, pushing her passion still higher. They
moved downward, curving around her bottom, pulling her toward him. He shifted his weight so that his

body covered hers. Her arms went around his neck, pulling him still closer. Her body arched up against his, fitting itself against him. It had been so long, so very long.

Then suddenly he was gone. She opened her eyes, wondering what he was going to do, and saw him on his knees beside her. His eyes gleaming in the soft light, he ran a hand lightly over her body, traced the swell of a breast, the curve of a hip, the flat plane of her stomach. She lay still, relaxed, yet with every nerve and cell alert for his touch.

Rivers of warmth flowed from his fingers, ran through her flesh. She was melting, turning soft and pliable under his hands.

His mouth followed his fingers, inflaming her even further, and a moan struggled from her lips. She twisted, her body wanting to escape his, yet only to get closer to it. She moved against him, trying to position her body nearer his. He laughed, a low throaty chuckle, deep and warm. "Patience," he whispered. "Patience, my love."

She was beyond speech, beyond anything but the need that possessed her. And then, when she thought she would explode from the pressure of the pleasure building inside her, she felt his body covering hers once again. She wrapped her arms around his neck, pulling him down against her. Her hands moved on his back, moved and clutched at empty air as he entered her. He moved against her, slowly at first, then harder and faster. Her body arched up to meet his. It was no longer a question of two bodies. Now they were one. One entity that moved and breathed and felt, together.

She clung to him, her hands clutching at his shoulders, as the waves of pleasure roared over her, carrying her higher and higher. Ecstasy flooded through her, filling her whole body with joy, and then he collapsed against her, and she heard, against her ear, his muffled exclamation.

The minutes passed, she didn't quite know how; she was still floating in a joyful haze. He rolled to one side, taking her with him, her head against his shoulder, where she drifted off to sleep.

She didn't know how long it was before she came abruptly awake, startled to find herself lying against a warm male body.

"What is it?" Kerr asked softly.

"I . . . I was sleeping." She felt suddenly embarrassed. She couldn't stay the night in this man's room. "I have to go," she said. "Back to my suite."

She felt the momentary tightening of his muscles. "Now?"

She fought the sudden desire to stay there, secure in the curve of his arm. This was illusion—the security she felt here. She had to get back to reality, to the cold facts. She pushed herself away from him.

"I'll go with you," he said.

"No, no." Her voice echoed shrilly in her ears. She made it lower, calmer. "There's no need, Kerr." She was surprised at the feeling in her voice. "You're all warm and comfortable here." She smiled down at him. "After all, this hotel is my territory. I can get back to my rooms easily enough. Besides"—she glanced at her watch—"it's better that I go alone. At this time of night . . ." The words hung there.

He opened his mouth; she was sure he meant to protest, but all he said was "Okay, if you're sure."

"I am." She found her underwear and pulled it on, fastened her bra. She considered carrying her panty hose and shoes, but if someone saw her . . . She sat down and pulled them on, conscious of his eyes. She slid the half-slip over her head, pulled it down around her hips, and stepped into her dress. Pulling it up over her shoulders, she backed toward the bed. "Will you zip me up?"

"Sure."

His fingers were cool against her skin as he found the zipper, but they heated her body, heated it with the remembrance of the things they had done. "There you are," he said.

She turned. There was no use prolonging this moment, no sense at all in wishing to crawl back into the bed with him. "Thank you, Kerr, for a lovely evening."

The expression on his face was unreadable, but his voice was warm. "Thank you, Amber," he said simply.

His hand closed around hers and for a moment she wondered if he meant to try to keep her there. But he released it when she turned toward the door.

"Good night, Amber." She wished he wouldn't say her name that way, that way that made shivers race up and down her spine.

"Good night, Kerr." She forced herself to cross the

room, to open the door and leave him. She didn't look toward him again as she softly closed the door.

The hall, fortunately, was empty and she hurried away toward the safety of her room, where she took off the clothes she had just put on and fell into bed. Yes, she thought with contentment, she had made the right decision. It wouldn't last—this deep feeling of fulfillment and satisfaction. It never lasted. But for tonight, well, this little piece of reality had been considerably brightened. And who could say. Maybe, just maybe, Kerr *was* right. Maybe reality *was* as you made it.

8

The shrill ringing of the phone woke Amber in the morning. Sunlight was visible, even through the heavy drapes, as she picked up the receiver. "Good morning."

"Good morning, beautiful."

Her body responded to the sound of his voice and warmth flooded over her. "Hello, Kerr."

"I hope I didn't wake you."

"No. Yes." She laughed. "It doesn't matter."

"It's still rather early, but I didn't know if you'd be working today."

"No, I'm not." She stretched, feeling the satisfaction in her body.

"How about breakfast?" Kerr was saying. "And, then, if you're not busy, we might take a look in the art gallery again. Sort of say good-bye to our favorites."

Yes, her mind cried. She wanted to see that picture of Pegasus again. If she had her own place . . .

She stopped the thought. "Okay. I'll meet you in the restaurant in half an hour."

"I'll be waiting."

Something in his voice stirred her body to more memories of the night before and she flushed, feeling the heat flooding her flesh. "See you there."

She put the phone back in its cradle and stretched again. It was great to wake up like this. She hadn't felt so good for a very long time. In fact, she wondered if she had ever felt so good.

Ten minutes later she was out of the shower, trying to decide what to wear. She felt far too relaxed for the formality of a suit. Finally she chose a pair of pale green slacks and a matching short-sleeved cotton sweater. They might be leaving the hotel and Memphis in May could be very warm. Her hair shimmered against the green as she brushed it. For a moment she considered not letting it hang free. But Kerr liked it that way. She made a little face at herself. So did she. She decided to let it hang. After all, she wasn't working today.

Kerr rose from his seat as she entered the restaurant. His face was one big smile. "Good morning." He dropped his voice. "You must have slept well last night. You look positively radiant."

She found herself grinning like a kid. "Yes, I did. Very well."

"Me, too." His eyes were warm. Pools of desire, they spoke eloquently to her of the night before.

Embarrassed by her body's quick reaction, she shifted her gaze to the menu. "Are you hungry?"

Again, there was that shared smile of mischief. And desire. "Ravenous. I understand the breakfast buffet is pretty good here."

She wondered why her lips insisted on curving into a smile. "Yes, it is."

He fingered his dark beard. "Then I guess I'll try that. You, too?"

"Yes, me, too."

If the waitress who took their orders was surprised to see the manager with such an attractive man, she kept herself from showing it. Amber was pleased. She liked a staff that functioned smoothly. She had no doubt, though, that the entire hotel staff would soon know about this breakfast. It didn't matter, really. What she did was her own concern. And it wouldn't hurt her image any to be seen with such an attractive man. She recognized this thought with some surprise. She was not accustomed to thinking in such terms.

The breakfast buffet was delicious. They ate for a while in comfortable silence. After Kerr had finished, he leaned back and sipped his second cup of coffee. "So," he said, "has your opinion of science fiction people been changed any?"

"Yes." She couldn't help another little smile.

"So, we're not all weirdos running around in capes and shooting one another with water pistols."

"It would appear not," she said, sipping her own coffee and trying to look businesslike. She had to admit that she had had no complaints from the other hotel guests. Not even about the game of Assassin, which had been played the previous night, while she and Kerr were out at dinner. "This group seems very well-behaved."

His grin made him look devilish. "Except for Holden."

Amber frowned thoughtfully. "Mr. Holden and his kind can be found in any group of people. I can hardly blame science fiction for him."

"And what about me?" he asked.

His eyes met hers and she could almost feel his hands on her again. Her blood grew warm. She only hoped it wasn't showing on her face, this rush of desire that he could evoke just by looking at her. "What about you?"

He shrugged. "In a certain sense I'm a product of science fiction."

"I don't understand. You're real. You're not made-up."

His face took on a quizzical look. "In a way we're all made-up. Every one of us."

"Now you're talking some kind of philosophical nonsense," she protested. "I'm real. So are you."

"But which you *are* you?" he asked, leaning toward her. "Are you the Amber *you* think you are? Or the one *I* think you are?"

She shook her head. "It's not a question of thinking at all. I am Amber Sinclair. And that's it."

Kerr shook his head. "That's not it. There are a lot of Ambers. The one I was with last night . . ." His voice dropped a tone and grew more intimate. "That was one Amber. The hotel manager is another. The wife you used to be, the daughter you are . . ." He looked at her steadily. "I could go on and on."

"Those are not different Ambers," she returned. "They're just pieces of me—parts of a whole." Except, she added silently to herself, the one you saw last night. She was made-up, created for the occasion, though I'd like to have her come back.

Kerr threaded his hands together. His fingers were dark, too, long and slender, yet very masculine. She felt a quiver of desire.

"I'm willing to concede that they're pieces of you," he said, his voice grave. "But there isn't any *real* you. No solid, unchangeable Amber. You change. From minute to minute, from second to second, Amber Sinclair changes."

She tried to digest this. It was an interesting theory, but that was all.

"Take me, for instance. What do you see when you look at me?"

"A man." The words came from her slowly, reluctantly. "A tall, dark, lean man. Attractive."

He smiled slightly. "That's the Kerr you know. The one I know is different. He's sometimes shy, sometimes frightened. Sometimes he believes he's not attractive at all."

She shook her head. "How could you believe that?"

He didn't smile at her compliment. "When I was young, I was afraid of girls."

She thought he must be kidding, but his face and his voice were deadly serious. "I mean it," he said. "I was so scared I couldn't even talk to a girl. I was gangly, kind of a beanstalk." He nodded as her eyes went to the breadth of his shoulders, to the well-muscled arms she knew his shirt concealed. "Yes, I know how I look now. But in a very real sense I *made* the Kerr you see today. I worked out and built up my body. I learned to take control of my life."

"I don't see . . ." she began.

"I could have gone on the way I was," he went on. "Awkward and clumsy. I could have gone on like that and blamed it all on life. And how far would that have gotten me?"

She could see the sense in that. Sort of. "But . . . but there are things that can't be changed. People are born with handicaps that can't be overcome."

He shook his head. "There are handicaps that can't be fixed," he said. "But there's no handicap that can't be overcome. At least in the sense that we have control over how we feel about it. Attitude is the secret," he continued. "Attitude is what makes our lives what they are."

Amber frowned. "What you say sounds great, but—"

"When you were with your husband, were things very bad?"

"No. Yes. I guess so." She felt confused, as though any answer she gave would be the wrong one.

"Did you think about how bad they were?"

She tried to remember. "Not most of the time."

"And after he left?"

"Then I knew how bad they had been." She couldn't see what he was trying to get at.

"But they were bad before?" He reached across the table to cover her hand with his in a comforting gesture.

"Yes." She tried to pull her hand away, but he held on to it.

"Then, it wasn't reality that changed," he pointed out. "It was your perception of it."

She couldn't refute this. It was true. "But . . ."

"It's all in your attitude," he repeated, stroking her hand before he released it. "Just think about it."

She finished off her own coffee. He could be so irritating sometimes. He was so sure he was right. Yet he wasn't smug about it. It was almost as though she were a small child, a small child to whom he was patiently and gently trying to explain something.

But she was not a child. And, much as she might want to believe, she couldn't. Facts were facts, however one might try to twist them. And the fact was that the world was a hard place. Attitude had nothing to do with it. Or at least, very little.

He pushed back his chair. "Well, shall we go take a look in the art gallery again?"

"Yes." She didn't want to argue with him. His words sounded good, very good, but she couldn't allow herself to believe them, much as she might want to, much as she did want to.

He paid the check and, fingers on her elbow, guided her toward the room set aside as the art gallery. There were a few new pieces, she noticed, but she gave them only a cursory look, her eyes going immediately to *her* Pegasus. The thought rather shocked her. The picture wasn't hers and never would be. The minimum bid was $20.00. She could not justify an expense like that, not for something that wasn't even useful.

For some reason her thoughts went to the amber paperweight on her desk. How could she put a price on what that paperweight had meant to her? She couldn't, of course, but that still didn't mean she could rationalize buying the Pegasus.

"It is beautiful," Kerr said. "I understand why you like it. Are you going to bid for it? There's an auction this afternoon at two. That'll be the last official event of the Mem-Con."

She shook her head. "No, I'm not going to bid on it. It doesn't belong in my world." The words startled her and she laughed, a brittle little laugh. "Now you've got me talking like you do," she said.

His smile warmed her blood and she felt the sudden yearning of her body toward his. "I'm glad. Hang around with me long enough and your attitude will change, too."

She shook her head. "I'm afraid you're wrong there." She looked at him carefully, wanting, she discovered, to understand him, to help him. "I don't see how you can believe the things you talk about," she said. "I mean, you're a grown man."

"Einstein was a grown man," he said quietly. "He believed things that had never been thought of before. And now we accept them as truth."

She frowned. "What you say sounds good. All that stuff about attitude sounds great. But it's just talk. When you get right down to it, the world is a cold, unfeeling place. Isn't it better to recognize that? To learn to live with it?"

"No." He said the word firmly as he led her toward the door and out into the corridor. "Can we continue this discussion while we walk back to our rooms? I need to pick up my notes for the next panel."

"Of course. I have things to do, too. But why do you tell me no?"

"Because it is a question of attitude. Take a rose, for instance. It has both blossoms and thorns. It depends on which you want to look at."

"But if you ignore the thorns, pretend they aren't there, you'll just get pricked." Why couldn't he see these simple things?

He shrugged. "If you're looking at the flower, you won't feel the prick so much. Life is like that. There are lots of blossoms hidden among the thorns. Like last night."

They were alone in the corridor and he pulled her to him for a brief kiss. Taken by surprise, she allowed it for a moment, relishing the feel of him against her. Then, recalling where they were, she drew back. "Someone might see us," she said hurriedly as she moved on.

He shrugged. "So what? There's no law against kissing, is there?"

She kept her voice firm and her feet moving. It was hard to resist him when he smiled like that. "I suppose not. But it surely wouldn't look good for the hotel's manager to be found kissing a guest in the hall."

He frowned, but the twinkle was still there in his eyes. "I think it depends on who finds them."

She couldn't help grinning back at him. Life did look different when he was around. "You must have

118

been very lucky in your childhood," she said, "to have such a sunny disposition."

But the twinkle faded. "'Afraid not, Amber. My childhood is best not discussed. Enough to say I was lonely and miserable. Clear into my teens. Until I decided to quit complaining about my life and take control of it."

She pushed absently at a wisp of hair that had fallen onto her forehead. "You can't take control of your life. There are too many variables."

"All the more reason to control what you can. And to remember that you can control your attitude."

"Back to that again," she said with a trace of exasperation.

"Yes." He smiled ruefully. "I'm afraid I've been preaching. I get carried away sometimes."

They had reached her door and she stopped, almost automatically. "Thank you for breakfast," she said.

"Thank *you.*" He glanced at her door. "Why don't you come to the noon seminar with me?" he said. "Three writers are going to talk about the future of science fiction."

Amber took her key from her pocket. "I'm afraid not, Kerr. I have some things to do today. But thank you." Mindful of where they stood, she extended her hand. For a long moment he simply stared at it. Then he reached out and took it between his own.

"I've got to check out this afternoon, so I may not see you before I leave." He hesitated. "Last night was beautiful," he said, his voice a husky whisper.

She nodded. That was true enough.

"I'd like to see you again," he went on. "I'd like to get to know you better."

Her heart began to pound in her throat, almost choking her so that she couldn't say anything; she knew she'd been waiting for those precious words. She forced her mouth to open. "Yes, I'd like that."

He smiled. "Good. I'll give you a call next week. We'll have some great adventures. Oh, keep your costume safe. We might need it again." His eyes gleamed. "Unless you'd like to dress like the maiden warrior I showed you."

She felt the blood rush to her cheeks. She could never go out in that state of near nudity! "I don't think . . ." she began.

"Don't think, love," he said softly. "Just feel." And he gathered her into his arms and kissed her soundly. She didn't debate with herself about returning his kiss. Her response was automatic.

When he finally put her from him, he smiled gently. "'Bye."

"'Bye." She watched him go, her bottom lip between her teeth, while her body yearned to hurry after him, to spend a few more precious hours in his company.

But she had to have time, she told herself as she entered her room. Time to think, time to examine the facts. She couldn't afford to get swept off her feet again, to suffer another Andy.

An hour later Amber sighed in exasperation and got up from her chair to pace her small living room. She couldn't seem to settle down to anything. She wanted to go search out Kerr, but that was one thing she wouldn't do, she told herself firmly.

Her mind presented her with such a vivid picture of Kerr's face that for a moment her steps faltered. Making an annoyed sound in her throat, she grabbed up her key and hurried out of her suite. What she needed was a good brisk walk.

But her steps took her, somehow, past the Hucksters' Room. And, though she really had no intention of stopping there, she found herself once more wandering up and down the crowded aisles.

She did not look around to see if Kerr was in the room. She knew somehow that he was not. Briefly she considered how this could be so—how she could know such a thing. But she had no answer to her question.

A display of calendars caught her eye and she stopped to browse. Browsing, after all, cost nothing; and her restlessness seemed to have eased since she'd come in here. She picked up one of the calendars and smiled in spite of herself. There was no need to read the bold print that proclaimed this a Boris Vallejo calendar.

It was all there in the female figure—primevally feminine and yet clearly strong and independent, able to take care of herself. Perhaps she needed such a calendar, Amber thought, to serve as a visual reminder that she was as strong and independent as . . . "Elizabeth-my-love." The words floating so clearly through her mind startled her, almost made her turn to see if Kerr were there beside her. She shook her head. She was not Elizabeth. And she was not Kerr's love.

She pushed the thought aside and opened her purse. Living as frugally as she had been, she deserved a little . . . She stopped herself short. This calendar wasn't for amusement. It was a very serious thing. A visual reminder to herself that she could be strong and independent. And she didn't have to run off into some imaginary world to do it, either. She could be—she was—strong and independent right in this world of reality. Most important of all, she didn't need a man to make her world complete.

She paid for the calendar and tucked the bag under her arm. Time now for that walk. But she didn't want to carry the bag with her. She decided to stop by her office first and leave the calendar there. On the way she passed the room that had been set aside for the art display. A quick glance at her watch told her that there was still some time before the art auction. And the next thing she knew she was going inside for a last look at her Pegasus.

He was still there, his strong wings looking somehow fragile and delicate against the azure sky. She sighed as her eyes lingered, trying to impress the image on her brain, trying to keep something of this beauty in her mind. Unconsciously her hand went to her purse and she began mentally to count her money. Maybe . . . When awareness of what she was doing hit her, the tears came suddenly, half blinding her, and she had to bite her bottom lip to keep them from spilling over and slipping down her cheeks. As quietly as she could, she slipped from the room and out into the hall.

She could not buy that print of Pegasus. It was

beautiful, but that was just the problem. It was too beautiful to be true. Just like last night, like all the time she had spent with Kerr. It was only when she was close to him that beauty seemed possible. And then it was like a dream. And that dream, she told herself ruthlessly, could not possibly come true, no matter what promises Kerr had made her. She didn't dare let herself hope. By the end of today the Pegasus, and all he symbolized, would be gone from the hotel. And from her life.

9

~~~~~~~~~~~~~~

The package arrived in the middle of the next afternoon. Betsy, her eyes brimming with curiosity, brought it into Amber's office. "This came for you, Mrs. Sinclair."

Amber looked up from the paper she had been studying. "I'm not expecting any packages. Where is it from?"

Betsy shook her head. "There's no return address. But it's clearly for you. The local delivery service brought it."

Amber frowned. "I can't think what it could be."

"Why don't you open it and find out?" suggested the eager and ever practical Betsy.

Amber nodded. She'd had trouble concentrating all day and she was behind in her work. But wondering about this mysterious package certainly would not help her to concentrate. She had a quick picture of another package, the costume Kerr had given her, packed up in its box and shoved deep into the back of her closet. Late the previous night she had made up her mind to waste no more time on foolish dreaming. Too bad, she thought as she took the package from Betsy's hand, that out of sight was not really out of mind.

The brown paper wrapping came away, revealing something rectangular, swathed in white tissue paper. Amber's hands kept moving, unwinding the paper from what was obviously a framed picture. Finally the wrappings lay across her desk and she stared down at the Pegasus print, now matted and very attractively framed.

"Oh! I wonder who sent it." Betsy's exclamation recalled Amber to her senses and she reached for the card taped to the back of the picture. Her eyes scanned it quickly. TO BEAUTY AND IMAGINATION, he had written. MAY THEY NEVER DIE. AND TO THAT DIFFERENT REALITY THAT WE SHARED. IF ONLY BRIEFLY. She stuffed the note back in its envelope and shoved it hastily into her pocket. "A thank-you gift," she improvised quickly. "From the Mem-Con."

Betsy's eyes twinkled. "I'll bet Mr. Corrigan was behind this," she said and sighed dramatically. "What a hunk of man."

Amber found herself unable to form a reply to this, but fortunately Betsy didn't notice. The young secretary had already swung around and was studying the room. "Now, let's see. Where shall we hang it?"

Amber knew she didn't want that picture hanging in

here, always under her eyes. It would be impossible to keep her hopes from rising every time she looked at the Pegasus. But she saw too late that she had made another mistake. Her evasion of where it had come from meant she couldn't send it back. Or even bury it in some closet like her costume. That could never be explained to Betsy.

She managed to pull herself together and get to her feet. "Let me see." For several minutes she pretended to study the room. Then she turned to Betsy and said brightly, "I've found the perfect spot."

"You have? Where?"

"Right there. Behind my desk. Then everyone can see it as they come into the room."

Betsy was silent for a moment, digesting this. When she spoke, it was clear she wasn't completely convinced. "Well, yes, but that way *you* can't see it."

That, thought Amber silently, was the whole idea. But she also thought it prudent to say aloud, "I can always turn my chair around. Besides, I'm supposed to be working in here, not contemplating paintings."

Betsy regarded the picture again. "It sure is pretty. How do you suppose they knew that it would go so well with your office?" She grimaced. "That Mr. Holden couldn't have told them." Her wrinkled nose made her feelings about the man quite visible. "That man has no taste at all. I think I must be right. It must have been that nice Mr. Corrigan."

Amber's hands had begun to tremble and she hid them quickly behind her. It was impossible to stop the rush of pleasure and anticipation that filled her when she thought of Kerr buying the print for her. But she mustn't get her hopes up. "Time to get back to work, Betsy. Will you call and have a man come hang the picture?"

"Of course, Mrs. Sinclair."

By the end of the week Amber was bitterly regretting the excited anticipation she'd felt Monday afternoon. The days had dragged like weeks and as Friday drew to a close it seemed to Amber that months had passed since she'd seen Kerr. It seemed certain that he hadn't really meant to call her. Her original decision to put him out of her mind had been a sound one. If only she hadn't let the Pegasus start her dreaming again!

For the thousandth time Amber asked herself why he had sent the print if he didn't mean to continue their relationship. Was it just his way of saying thank you for their night together? Had their lovemaking been nothing more than a fantasy escape for him?

Whatever the reason, it looked like Kerr hadn't meant the things he'd said. She didn't like to believe that. She didn't like to think that he was a liar. But then, didn't those people lie all the time, in a sense, with their crazy make-believe worlds? He had just lied a little more.

She reached for the top file folder. This had to stop. There was work— The shrilling of the phone startled her and she tried to calm herself. There was no point in being so jumpy every time it rang; Kerr wasn't going to call.

The light on her phone indicated that the call was for her. With a trembling hand Amber picked up the receiver. "Hello. Amber Sinclair speaking."

"Hello, beautiful."

The breath caught in her throat. She would know that voice anywhere.

"Good afternoon, Mr. Corrigan."

His laughter was warm; it tingled down her spine. "Why so formal, my love?"

Obviously Kerr hadn't guessed that his failure to call earlier would upset her. "This is a business office," she replied, managing to get a little crispness into her tone. She couldn't let him know how absurdly relieved she was to hear his voice.

"Of course. I get it. Someone's there. Listen, love. I'll make it short. I just got in from the West Coast; been gone all week. I'm still at the airport, in fact. And I'm dying to see you. Give me a while to wash up. I'll be at your door at seven sharp. 'Bye."

With a sense of shock Amber realized that he had already hung up. Dazedly she put the phone back in its cradle. Thoughts tumbled through her mind, mad chaotic thoughts. He *had* meant to call her; he'd just been away. And he seemed to think there was something special between them. Just as she had, a part of her mind reminded her, until her own self-doubt had undermined her belief that there could be something wonderful between them.

Getting your hopes up again, chided the dry voice in her head that always chortled over her mistakes. You know that will only lead to disappointment in the end.

But for once Amber ignored that dry, cautionary voice. This time, she told herself, I'm going to do what *I* want to do. I'm going to give Kerr a chance.

And with that she turned back to her papers, determined to accomplish something in the hour she had left to work.

Later, in her room, she was a bundle of nerves. She didn't know how she was going to behave with him. And what should she wear? Kerr hadn't given her any inkling of what he had in mind for the evening.

She raced around the small suite, flicking away imaginary dust and smoothing cushions until she came abruptly to her senses and made herself sit down and relax. She was behaving very foolishly.

But no matter how much she scolded herself, she couldn't forget the sound of his voice saying "Hello, beautiful"; saying "Listen, love."

She got to her feet again and headed for the closet. Why hadn't she bought something new? Something besides the subdued colors she had thought appropriate for work?

And then she thought of it—the dress of off-white that she had picked up last year. Made of lightweight chiffon, it would do just fine for a June evening. She pulled it out of the back of the closet and stood looking at it. It was the style she liked—long full sleeves, a soft bodice, and a full swirly skirt.

It was obviously not practical, but she had justified its expense because even a working wardrobe needed something frivolous for the occasional office get-together.

She glanced at her watch: still an hour until he would be there. She hung the dress in the front of the closet and turned toward the bathroom. A leisurely bath would relax her.

On an impulse she poured in a generous helping of the bubble bath that had been Betsy's Christmas present to her. Usually she didn't care for such things, but tonight was different and it wasn't as though the stuff had cost her anything.

Sinking into the warm bubbles, she smiled. They *were* relaxing. There was really no sense getting so nervous about this date with Kerr. He was just another man. And she was certainly entitled to a little relaxation.

That dry voice in her head reminded her somewhat caustically that it was not just "a little relaxation" that she was preparing for. Her body was already busy remembering his, her flesh trembling in anticipation of his touch.

She closed her eyes and tried to conjure up images of relaxation. But the screen of her mind showed her nothing but pictures of Kerr. As she had first seen him in costume, across the Hucksters' Room; as he had looked in his suit across the little table in the restaurant; and finally, though she tried to prevent that, as he had lain naked beside her in the bed.

The warm water seemed suddenly chill, and gooseflesh stood out on her skin. Would he want to go to bed with her tonight? It had certainly sounded that way. She sighed. Her body was more than ready for his. But was this the right thing to do?

They were so different in their approaches to life. How could anything permanent come of their relationship? The thought of permanency was only a minor shock to her. She was not, after all, the kind of woman who went blithely from man to man. There had been no one before Andy. No one after. Until now.

But Kerr Corrigan, her mind chided her, Kerr Corrigan was just too different, too unrealistic.

Yet Amber was forced to admit that his attitude didn't appear to have hurt him. He seemed very successful in his career. And very intelligent, surely. She didn't know much about quantum physics, but she could hardly escape knowing that a person didn't become a physicist overnight. Such a career took a lot of hard work and the brains to do it.

The bathwater grew cool as Amber lay there, reliving the time she had spent with Kerr. Finally she glanced at the clock and got to her feet. Time to finish getting ready.

The texture of the towel as she dried herself was disconcerting. Her body seemed to have wakened from a deep sleep. Like Sleeping Beauty, said the caustic voice in her mind. Except that "happily ever after" was only for fairy tales.

With another sigh, Amber pulled the pins from her French knot. Her hair fell to her shoulders in shimmering waves. As she brushed it she debated with herself: Should she put it up again or should she leave it down? Actually, said another part of her mind, a joyous laughing part that she hardly recognized, it would be coming down anyway when they made—She shut off that thought. She would leave it down because that style suited the dress better. That was reason enough.

She finished her makeup and slipped into her

clothes. The bone-colored sandals she chose had medium heels, in case they decided to walk somewhere. But they also went very well with the dress.

Surveying her image in the mirror, Amber felt a little sense of shock. She didn't look like herself at all. The sober businesswoman had disappeared. This woman with the sparkling eyes seemed almost radiant. She turned away with another sigh. She was behaving like a fool. One night with a man wasn't going to change her whole life. And yet, whispered that romantic part of her mind that she had not yet succeeded in taming, it just might. Such things had happened.

The rap on the door came just at that moment and she turned to open it with relief. No more internal debates. At least, not right now. When Kerr was with her, everything seemed right.

She opened the door and stood there trembling.

"Hello, love." His voice caressed her and his eyes . . . his eyes took her immediately back to the night she had spent in his arms.

"He—hello, Kerr."

He was wearing a summer-weight beige suit that set off his dark good looks. A shiver of desire ran down her spine. "C—come in."

As she stepped back she wondered why she'd done that. There was no reason to invite him into her suite. Except that she wanted to see him there. "I'll just get a wrap. The air-conditioning in some places can be too cold."

He nodded and stepped inside, his eyes never leaving her.

"I—I didn't know what you had in mind for tonight," she began, then flushed as she realized this wasn't exactly the truth. "That is, I hope I'm dressed all right."

His warm laughter filled the room. "Actually, what's most on my mind requires no clothes at all." His eyes twinkled at her. "But I thought you might like dinner first. You haven't eaten yet, have you?"

"No." She couldn't respond to the invitation in his eyes, not the way she wanted to, not by running into his arms and raising her mouth for his kiss. Something inside, something cautionary, held her back.

He looked around the rooms. "These don't look much like you. No imagination."

"I told you . . ." she began, but his smile stopped her.

"Don't bother to deny it, love." He held out a small package and she realized she hadn't even noticed he was holding something. "Some new reading material. A couple of my very favorites."

She took the steps that brought her closer to him, but he put the package on an end table.

"So you put the Pegasus in your bedroom," he said with obvious satisfaction.

Amber took a deep breath and wet her lips. "Actually, it's hanging in my office."

He considered this for a moment, then his smile deepened. "I think I like that even better. Ready?"

She took her wrap, lifted her purse from the table, and moved toward him. "Yes."

He did then what she had been longing to do since the moment she saw him. He covered the rest of the distance that separated them and took her in his arms.

His mouth was warm against hers and she yielded herself to his kiss, her body curving to fit against his, her blood singing in her veins.

When he released her mouth, she felt almost too weak to stand, but his arm remained around her. "Now, that's the way a man should be welcomed home. With a kiss from his woman."

10

They did eat dinner, though afterward she had only the haziest memory of the place and the food. Her whole body was waiting for what his eyes promised.

They didn't linger over coffee. She refused dessert. Her stomach was tying itself in knots of anticipation and her throat was dry.

He leaned across the little table and covered her hand with his. "I think you know what's on my mind, love. I'd like to take you back to my place. I've a lot of science fiction fantasy art you might enjoy." His eyes twinkled and his voice deepened. "I've got something else for you, too. Something I've been saving all week."

She tried to think of something witty to say, but all she could think of was her need, her need to be in his arms, to be held against his loving body. "I . . . I'd like that."

Moments later he was backing the car out of the restaurant parking lot. "I live out in Germantown," he said. "In a condo."

"Do you like it?" She was desperately trying to make conversation.

"Yes," he said. "I like it. But come over here closer to me. I missed you something dreadful this week." He turned a searching gaze on her face. "I hope you missed me."

Amber thought of the long days and even longer nights, of the hundred and more times she had pivoted her office chair to gaze at that ethereal Pegasus and the hope he promised. "Yes," she said. "I missed you."

"Good." His satisfaction was evident. "I'm glad."

He took her fingers in his strong brown ones and desire danced through her body; danced madly and wildly.

Fortunately the ride to his place didn't take long. She was conscious of the studied elegance in the lobby and halls, but when they reached his suite she could think of nothing but the man himself. He switched on the lights and locked the door behind them. Her wrap and purse fell from her lifeless fingers as he came toward her, his face burning with desire. And then she was in his arms.

This kiss lasted longer than their first. Her body curved itself eagerly to fit against his and her arms went automatically around his neck. His lips were soft and persuasive. Like some narcotic drug, they erased all sense from her mind, completely silenced the cautionary voice that was trying to warn her, and dissolved her bones so that she had to cling to him for support.

When he released her mouth, he sighed deeply. "Talk about the subjective quality of time! This must have been the longest week in my entire life!"

"Mine, too." She was hardly conscious of what she was saying or of the fact that she had agreed with his strange concept of time. All she could think of was the feel of his strong body against hers, of the desire that was spiraling within her.

He looked down at her, his dark eyes gleaming. "Now that we've had dinner and observed the amenities, maybe we can dispense with the behavior of civilized people."

She reached up to put a kiss on the point of his soft beard. At that moment, with his arms around her, her body melting into his, she would have agreed to almost anything. Still, she asked "What do you mean?"

"I mean," he replied, kissing her forehead, "that when you opened your door for me tonight, my first impulse was to become a caveman, to rip off this pretty dress and get to the woman underneath."

His laugh was deep and warm. "But I subdued my baser instincts," he went on, "and took you to dinner first."

"And now?" she prompted, only vaguely aware of how unlike her usual self she was behaving.

"Now, I'd like to follow my first impulse. Well," he conceded, "the dress is too pretty to rip off, but I bet I could get you out of it in a hurry."

She smiled up at him, her fingers stroking the nape of his neck under the dark curly hair. "Why don't you, then?" she asked with mock innocence.

This time his laughter rang out, echoing through the room. "You mean you're not really interested in seeing my art collection?"

"You forget," she said, keeping her innocent tone, "I don't even like science fiction."

"Of course." His eyes twinkled while he tried to look properly abject. "How rude of me." The arms that held her tightened. "But I do know something you like."

He swung her up into his arms so swiftly that she squealed in alarm. "And I'm going to give you a lot of it."

And with that he carried her across the living room and pushed open a door. Even in her preoccupation with him, Amber couldn't help noticing the room. Half a dozen Boris heroines decorated the walls and the one he had said reminded him of her, the red-haired female warrior on a horse, hung in a place of honor opposite his bed.

"You see," he said, carrying her to the bed. "You belong in here."

The words started a warmth deep inside her, a warmth that had nothing to do with the way her body was responding to his. But she couldn't think about it then; she would save it for later.

He put her on the bed and sat down beside her, his

eyes gleaming with mischief. "Or maybe I've got a better idea."

Her heart was pounding now and she almost reached up to pull him down on top of her. "Yes, what?"

"We'll have a race. Whoever gets completely undressed first and hits the bed wins."

"Wins what?" she asked, laughing.

Warm fingers stroked her cheek. "Whatever he or she wants," he said softly, his voice as tender as his fingers. "Okay?"

"Okay."

She was vaguely aware that this whole thing was childish, that properly mature people surely didn't do such things. But the part of her mind that was in control really didn't care. When Kerr grinned and said "go!" her fingers flew just as rapidly as his and her laughter bubbled just as freely.

When moments later they tumbled naked together into his bed and reached for each other, Kerr cried, "I won!"

"You didn't!" she retorted. "I hit the bed the same time you did."

"Then," he said, gathering her close against him. "I guess we'll have to take turns. Agreed?"

"Agreed." She lay on her side, her body half over his, her head fitting naturally into the hollow of his shoulder, her breasts pressing against his chest. She could feel the dark wiry hair there against the sensitive skin of her breasts; it seemed to fondle her already erect nipples. A deep sigh welled up in her throat.

"Comfortable?" he asked, his free hand making slow circles on her hip.

"Hmmmmm," she murmured, savoring the feel of his body against her own. For a moment she felt completely relaxed. But when his hand moved from her hip to trace lazy circles nearer and nearer the pink nipple that yearned for his touch, she felt the heightening of desire deep within her. Like storm clouds, desire gathered and billowed inside her. But they would not open and dispense the cool contentment of satisfaction until that magic moment when two became one.

Her left hand stroked his chest, gently touching the nipples almost lost in the dark tangle of hair; she stirred against him, tilting her head so that she could look into his eyes.

What she read there raised her desire even higher. Then his mouth came down on hers, at first light and teasing, then harder, more possessive. Her body changed, became molten, wanted to flow into his, to become as close to him as human anatomy would allow.

When he released her lips, they were both breathing deeply. "Ladies first," he whispered against her ear, his warm breath stirring her senses. "What would you like?"

She tried to get her thoughts together, to think of something she could ask him to do that he hadn't done before. And then it came to her. It was so wild an idea, so unlike her normal self, that she was amazed. But she still went on to ask him, "Tell me about our latest adventure, Zonan. What exciting things happened to us?"

For a moment the body so close to hers lay perfectly still and she wondered if she had offended him.

But then he spoke. "Yes, Elizabeth-my-love, I'll tell you."

For one of those rare times in her life Amber wished for a different name. She had always liked her name. It was different. It was beautiful. Of course she knew that beauty . . . She pushed the thought aside. For tonight she was Elizabeth and she just didn't care what the real world was like or if she was deceiving herself. Right at that moment, with Kerr's body so close to hers, logic and scientific thought meant less than nothing to her.

Kerr's hand continued its stroking as he talked. "Would you rather hear about the time I rescued you from the water serpents' lair or about the time we defeated the wicked king of Ardua?"

"Did we do that together?" she asked, planting a kiss on the side of his beard.

"Yes. We fought side by side."

"Good."

His hand continued to move as he spoke and her hands began their own exploration. "What was wrong with this king?" she asked, tangling her fingers in his chest hair. "Why did we have to fight him?"

"The usual thing," Kerr said, a hint of laughter in his voice. "He had too much power and it corrupted him. You know how power is. He lost all sense of justice and fairness. Raised the taxes to astronomical heights, conscripted all the men for his army, generally oppressed the people."

"I see. And did we take on this moral monster all

alone?" She ran her hand over the flat plane of his stomach, felt his flesh quiver in response.

"Of course, my love. It was our bounden duty. Though the people rallied round us when they saw our noble purpose."

Her hand moved farther down his stomach, to the top of his strong muscular thigh. "Of course. And did we achieve our noble purpose?" Her fingers went sideways, lightly touching his maleness, and he shivered again.

Suddenly his hand captured hers and returned it to his chest. "I think, my love, that you have missed your calling."

"How so?" She wanted to say 'my love' to him, but the words simply couldn't get past some block in her head.

"I believe you have a streak of cruelty. How you do torture a man."

She laughed. "Look who's talking." Her breath came in shortened gasps as his fingers searched for and found her most vulnerable place.

He laughed, too, and withdrew his hand. "Now, do you want the rest of this story, or do you want something else?" His fingers played with the smooth curve of her stomach.

"I want both," she said softly, her mouth against his throat. "First the story."

He sighed dramatically, but he went on. "The king tried to kidnap you, to use you as a hostage to bring us in line. But his lackeys failed in the attempt. So you and I crept into the palace one dark night."

"Through a secret passageway, no doubt." She heard the laughter in her voice with a sensation of surprise.

"Of course, my love. How else? And we put the fear of God into the king by convincing him that we were spirits and could get to him anytime we pleased. And so he reconsidered his ill-advised procedures and became a model king."

"My, my," she said. "We certainly have been busy."

"Yes, we have."

His quick movement took her by surprise. One moment he was lying there, his body against hers, and the next he was on his knees beside her. "And that is the end of the story," he said. "Now it's my turn."

"Yes," Amber agreed. The soft light in the room bathed him with mystery; made his face dark and shadowy. "What do you want me to do?"

"I warn you." His grin was wicked. "It's going to be really hard for you."

At the moment she felt that she could do anything. "Tell me. I'll do it."

"I want you to lie perfectly still."

"But . . ."

"I'm supposed to get what I want, aren't I?"

"Yes, but . . ."

"No buts about it. That's what I want. I want you to lie perfectly still." He grinned again. "Or as near that as you can manage."

She raised herself on one elbow to continue the conversation, but he pushed her back down on the bed, his lips seeking her breast; for a moment she forgot everything but the riot of feeling his busy mouth induced in her.

It had seemed like such a simple request. What could be easier than just lying there perfectly still? But with his mouth on her and desire coiling inside her, it was impossible to do. Her flesh yearned toward him, needing his touch. Whatever part of her body he fondled felt deserted when he moved on to another. Under the ministrations of his tongue she panted and squirmed, avid for his touch.

Finally she could stand it no longer and reached up to grab his shoulders and pull him down against her. "Please, please hold me for a minute."

He took her in his arms, their bodies fitting together perfectly. She sighed in contentment as her flesh met his.

She lifted her head from the hollow of his shoulder to smile dreamily. "I feel so good."

His laughter expressed delight while his hand went to her breast. "I agree, love. You feel *very* good."

For some reason this outrageous pun struck her as hilarious and she laughed there in his arms, her face against his.

"Love *is* good, isn't it?" he whispered, his tongue tracing the curve of her earlobe.

"Mmmmm." She was not quite as dreamy as she sounded. He had spoken of love and that warmed the secret places of her soul, places where even his physical caresses could not reach. And now, close beside him, she could silence the voice of caution, forget for a little the dry, uncaring universe. In Kerr's arms anything seemed possible and she wanted to revel in that very possibility. To let her imagination out of the darkness in which she had kept it imprisoned, to set it free to soar, like Pegasus, on ethereal wings.

"Penny?" he asked, his breath warm on her ear.

She didn't even consider avoiding his question or answering it with something else. "I was thinking about possibility," she whispered. "About Pegasus flying free."

The arms that held her to him tightened. "And imagination?" he asked softly, his lips brushing the pulse that beat in her throat.

"Yes." She felt no embarrassment at revealing her thoughts to him. "About that, too."

"I bet you have a good imagination," he continued, his fingers on her back, moving in a soft caress.

She remembered how she had denied it, telling him she had no imagination at all. So much had happened in the week since then. More, it seemed, than in all the time since her marriage had ended. "I don't know. I haven't used it much."

He nuzzled her neck. "I think what's more likely is that you've tried *not* to use it. But I bet you've had your share of daydreams, beautiful imaginings that even your parents couldn't stop."

"You're right," she whispered, running a fingertip over the line of his lips. But she didn't go on to tell him that lately, during this past week, all her imaginings had centered around him, around the hope that they could be together like this.

He wrapped a strand of her hair around his finger. "I love your hair," he said. "It's so long and silky.

145

Smooth. Like the rest of you." He released her hair and his fingers went to a rosy nipple. "Well, like most of the rest of you."

She laughed with him. She felt light-headed and giddy, but she didn't care. When she was with him, nothing else mattered. Everything was as it should be. Just as it should be.

"You know what?" he asked, nibbling delicately at the edge of her ear.

"No, what?"

"I've been thinking about this all week. About you and about our being together." He chuckled. "Especially about our being together in my bed."

It struck her then, the first thorn in this rose-blossom evening. How many other women had been in this room—in this bed—with Kerr? It was an uncomfortable thought, but it seemed lodged in her head.

"I've been a long time alone," he went on in a tone of recollection.

"But you're so attractive!" The words came from her without conscious thought. "How can that be?"

He smiled. "I guess I'm sort of a particular person. I know what I want in a woman. I want more than sex."

With me? she wanted to ask. Do you want more than sex with me? But her newfound freedom to express herself seemed to have deserted her and her tongue lay paralyzed in her mouth.

"I want a woman who can share my life," he went on. "Or maybe I should say 'lives.' Someone who can appreciate the fun of make-believe. Of different realities."

His hand moved on her hair, smoothing it out over

her shoulders. But she felt a chill inside. She was not like that, not like the woman Kerr wanted. She didn't—couldn't—see the world as he did, through rose-colored glasses.

She laughed, but this time the sound was definitely artificial. "Then what am *I* doing here?" She wanted to stop, to take back the words, to assure him that she did belong, right there in his arms. But something made her rush on. "You know I don't agree with your theories. You can't change reality just by wishing." *Oh, but I want to,* her heart cried. *I want to change it. I want to live in your world, my darling.*

He pulled her tighter against him. "I don't believe that," he said firmly. "Your imagination is there. It's just a little feeble because you haven't given it much exercise." He kissed her nose. "Besides, I fancy myself a hero. And you know that heroes are always rescuing maidens from monsters and such. Your monster is just a little more abstract than most." He chuckled. "It's big, though. Maybe I'm being silly to take on a whole universe, especially one as bad as yours." His lips brushed her cheeks. "Superman only had to turn back time by reversing the earth's rotation. But I have to deal with a whole universe full of precisely ordered molecules." His lips went to her forehead; left a light kiss there.

If anyone could do it, she thought, he could. But she couldn't say that.

"Speaking of molecules," he went on, "I think I'll just get to work on the collection I have right here, under my hand, so to speak."

As his hands and his mouth began to move again,

she could only lie there. There were many things she wanted to tell him. How she wanted to beg him not to give up, to keep after her until she *could* see things his way, until she *could* live in the same wonderful reality he did. But the words piled up in her throat and stuck there. And then, as his hands and mouth moved over her, passion reasserted itself and words became meaningless sounds, not nearly as important as the moans of joy he wrung from her.

He took his time, bringing her again and again to the very edge while she struggled to pull him toward her, to take that final spiraling ascent into joy that only their joining could bring her.

But still he resisted the arms she reached out to him. Her breath came in ragged gasps; her body twisted and turned in the big bed.

Finally when her whole self, body and mind, was one terrible ache for the feel of him, when she thought one more caress would be more than her sensitive body could bear, he lowered himself on her. Their very joining sent her off in spirals of delight and he lay quiet, allowing her to regain her breath, before he began to move against her, slowly, surely, with a rhythm that teased and tantalized her arching body.

His breath was hot against her ear. His arms under her shoulders gathered her to him. "I've dreamed of you," he whispered, his voice hoarse. "I've dreamed of you and I've been looking for you all my life. Now that I've found you . . ." He had to stop talking, to gulp great breaths of air. "Now that I've found you, I'm never going to let . . . you . . . go."

They reached it, then, and together they soared

over the edge, soaring upward in great circles of delight. As though, Amber thought through a haze of pleasure, as though Pegasus himself had lifted them to the heights. And then slowly, supported by the great white wings, they drifted back to Earth.

She had never felt so good, so satisfied, so complete, she realized, as he rolled off her and pulled her close to his side. And he *had* said that. She smiled to herself. Her imagination couldn't have come up with *that*, even in the heat of passion. He *had* said that he never wanted to let her go. She hugged that sentence to her, hiding it away in the recesses of her heart with other things he had said about the future. There *was* a chance for them to have a life together. A good chance.

11

On Monday morning when Amber returned to the office, the world seemed new. She knew it was the same old place. Nothing had really changed. Yet everything seemed different. Kerr would call her again this coming weekend he had said, warning her that the press of business might well take him out of town during the week, but assuring her that he would be back to spend the next weekend with her.

She could hardly believe it, but she had spent the whole weekend with him, not returning to the hotel until late Sunday evening. And now she moved in a haze of glory. Being with Kerr was so overpowering, so complete an experience, that nothing could compare to it.

When Betsy arrived, she found that Amber had moved the Pegasus from behind her desk to a position where it could be easily seen from her chair. Amber saw the girl's startled expression before she recovered. "I've decided he looks better over there," she explained airily and Betsy happily agreed.

The week flew by; even the most tiring jobs were made easier by the sight of the great white horse. Soon, Amber reminded herself, soon it would be Friday and Kerr would arrive to carry her to the heights again. Only she would not be too greedy. She would not try, like Bellerophon, to join the gods. She would not try to make this enchanted world hers forever. Though she would like—

Whenever her thoughts got that far, she quickly stopped them.

On Thursday Kerr called her from the airport. "Got to fly to the East Coast," he said. "But I'll be back tomorrow night. I'll come to you right from the plane." His chuckle was deep and rich. "I can shower later. With you."

His words brought the rush of hot blood to her cheeks and desire to her body, but fortunately there was no one in her office to see. "Great. I'll be ready," she answered.

Unlike the other days, Friday dragged. Now that the magic time was drawing closer, every second seemed an hour, but the day ended finally and she hurried to her suite to get ready. Some time after seven, Kerr had said. She showered and put on the new dress she'd bought, a pale peach silk creation with a wide swirling skirt and full sleeves. She brushed her hair till it crackled, and applied a little eye shadow and lipstick. Then she forced herself to settle into a chair and pick up the book she was currently reading. One of those that Kerr had brought her.

The story was fascinating—a fantasy in which a couple in love could experience each other's thoughts and feelings. More than once tears came to Amber's eyes. How beautiful such a love must be. In this world such telepathic contact was impossible. But what she felt for Kerr seemed somehow to approach it. There were times when his eyes spoke eloquently to hers and she seemed to know exactly what he was thinking. She smiled slightly. It wasn't always when he was thinking of sex, either.

A knock sounded on the door, and startled, she dropped the book into her lap. Her fingers seemed all thumbs as she picked it up and set it on the nearby table. Maybe he had taken an earlier plane.

She flew to the door, stopped for one last pat to her hair, and flung it open. It was hard to tell who felt the greater shock, Amber or the older couple who stood there.

When she finally pulled herself together and met her mother's eyes, they were wide with surprise. Could this creature be her daughter? they seemed to say. "Mother. Dad. What are you doing here?" They were not the most cordial words of welcome, but once spoken they couldn't be taken back.

Her mother was the first to recover herself. "We're taking a little trip out west to Denver," she said. "And we decided to see how you're doing."

"Oh. You should have let me know you were coming." She hoped the words didn't reveal how upset she was feeling. "How long do you have?"

"Just till tomorrow morning," her father said. "We wanted to see your new place."

Both of them were peering past her with undisguised curiosity. With an overwhelming feeling of regret she let go of her dreams for the evening. "Come on in," she said, trying to put more warmth into her voice than she felt.

"Are you sure we aren't keeping you from something?" her mother asked as she stepped in and looked around.

"I . . . ah . . . had plans for dinner," Amber explained, knowing that her mother would guess there was some reason she was so dressed up.

"Perhaps you can call the young man," her father suggested with an attempt at joviality. "Make it tomorrow evening."

Amber shook her head. There was nothing she would like more than to stop Kerr before he arrived at her suite to be examined by her parents like some laboratory specimen. But short of having him paged at the airport, she couldn't think of any way to do so. "I'm afraid not, Dad. I can't reach him."

Her mother's raised eyebrows made her hurry on. "He's been out of town." Somehow that didn't sound any better. In spite of her twenty-five years, in spite of her good job, in spite of everything she knew about herself and her abilities, she felt as she had as a child—like a little girl trying to understand a cold and frightening world. Her wonderful evening with Kerr was ruined before it ever began.

Her mind raced frantically. How could she get him to understand? How could she give him a way to ease out gracefully? Not many men, she thought wryly, would want to spend the evening entertaining her parents.

"Sit down," she said, but her words fell on unhearing ears. Her mother was already in the kitchen, opening doors, considering the arrangement of her cupboards. And her father had wandered over to the window and was looking down on the pool.

"Not a bad place," he commented. "Saves you a lot, I bet. You'll be getting a nice little nest egg put away."

"Yes, Dad." There was no point in telling them that she was saving for a place of her own, that she was tired of living in a hotel.

"Amber!" Her mother's slightly raspy voice came ringing from the kitchen. "What's this thing on the wall?"

Amber's heart rose up in her throat and before she could stop herself her glance went to the book on the end table. She knew what her mother had seen: the Boris Vallejo calendar that she had bought at Mem-Con and hung in her kitchen. She swallowed hastily. "That's a calendar, Mother."

"I can see that much. What I want to know is what it's doing in your kitchen."

Her father turned from the window. "Calendars are usually used to tell the date," he observed dryly. "Often find them in kitchens."

"This calendar," her mother replied, her voice rising an octave, "is almost indecent."

"Really? Let me see."

The speed with which her father made his way to

the little kitchen was not lost on Amber. This was a side of him she had never noticed before. She moved to join them.

"It's science fiction art, Mother," she explained. "This artist is a well-known illustrator."

Her mother's eyebrows went up again, but she said nothing more. If the man was a success, he obviously had something. But to find such a thing in her daughter's kitchen had been a shock to her. Her expression indicated she hoped that much was clear.

"I didn't know you read science fiction," her father had begun, when there was another knock on the door.

Amber felt her knees begin to tremble. If only Kerr would see how things were and leave quickly. She could handle her parents if he would just leave them alone. On shaky legs she went to the door.

"Hello, beautiful."

She longed to run into his arms, to shelter herself there, but she didn't dare. Instead she stood quietly, her eyes pleading with him to understand. "Hello, Kerr. I . . . I'm sorry. I won't be able to see you tonight. My parents came in unexpectedly. They're leaving again in the morning."

"Oh." He tried to look around her shoulder, but was unsuccessful. Why didn't he just go? For a moment she thought he might do that; then his eyes met hers and with a real sense of shock she read his thoughts there. He had no intention of leaving without meeting her parents.

In fact, his eyes gleamed with anticipation. "I never could turn my back on a challenge," he whispered for her ears alone. And then louder, so they could hear, "Why, darling, how wonderful! You know how I've been wanting to meet them."

And before she could think of anything to do, or say, he had swept past her into the room and was greeting two rather dazed people.

Her father recovered first. "Kerr. Kerr Corrigan," he repeated after Kerr introduced himself. "Seems I've seen that name just lately. What do you do?"

"I'm in physics, sir. Quantum physics."

Her father's face revealed incredulity, Amber saw, and her mother's mouth fell open. "I knew it," her father exclaimed. "I read about you the other day in one of the journals." He beamed. "You've made quite a name for yourself."

Kerr shrugged; his smile was deprecating. "Just doing my job, sir. Say, this is just great, your being in town like this. We can all go to dinner together."

"Well, now . . ." Her father seemed aware of Amber's hesitancy, but her mother was so charmed by Kerr that she could see nothing else. "That's a wonderful idea, Mr. Corrigan. We would enjoy seeing some of Memphis."

"Do call me Kerr," he said and glanced at his watch. "If I can just use your phone, Amber-love, I'll change the reservations."

She started to say "Of course" after she winced at his use of Amber-love, but he was already headed for the kitchen and the phone that hung there. She saw her parents exchange glances that said this man knew his way around their daughter's place very well.

Standing there, Amber began to fret. She knew

from firsthand experience how overpowering her parents could be. Hadn't they managed to stifle her imagination, to convince her that the world was as *they* saw it? Kerr was so vulnerable, with his belief in possibilities, in imagination. If he started talking about these things, her parents would ruin them for him.

To her surprise, she realized that she didn't want that to happen. She was beginning to like the world Kerr had built for himself, beginning to hope she might share it with him. But her parents would spoil all that. They would destroy his world and all the beauty he loved.

Her anxiety over this kept her more or less speechless as they drove downtown. But Kerr had things well in hand. He took a route that gave them a spectacular view of sunset on the Mississippi, just as though he didn't know that such a thing would not interest her parents. At least they had the politeness to seem suitably impressed, though she knew that sunsets, or the paddle-wheel steamers docked near the Pier restaurant, meant less than nothing to them.

"Too bad you don't have more time," Kerr said as he guided them toward the restaurant stairs. "A paddle-wheel ride is a real treat. There's nothing more relaxing."

Amber saw her parents exchange glances again and she could almost hear them thinking that relaxation was a waste of precious time. But they didn't say it.

When they were seated, Kerr managed to position himself beside Amber. She felt his leg brush against hers and turned to look at him. His eyes were bright and she realized that he was truly enjoying himself.

How that could be she couldn't begin to understand. Except for that one mistake with Andy, that one horrendous mistake, she had always taken the path of least resistance where her parents were concerned. They were iron-minded people and a decision once made by them had never in her experience been changed.

Now she watched in a sort of daze as Kerr cajoled her seafood-hating mother into trying the catch of the day and at the same time drew out her father about his job.

"I'm just an unimportant high school chemistry teacher," her father said. "Trying to pound the basics into a lot of unwilling heads."

Kerr's smile was charm itself. He missed his calling, Amber thought, making a mental note to tell him so later. He would have made a wonderful diplomat.

"Now, sir, you don't mean that. Without men like you our country would have no scientists. We wouldn't have gotten to the moon or done any of the other wonderful things we've accomplished in this century."

Amber saw her father look a little sheepish. And well he might, she thought, stifling an insane impulse to giggle. Here he was being given credit for what he had countless times called "the stupidest event" of the century. To her surprise, however, he smiled slightly and murmured, "You're too kind."

"No, sir, I'm not." Kerr wasn't going to let the matter drop. "High school science teachers are the backbone of this nation. Of course, some are sometimes a little behind the times." His knee brushed Amber's under the table, but his eyes never left her father's face.

"I remember a teacher of mine. Very set in his ways." Again that pressure of his knee told Amber that he knew exactly what he was doing. She managed, though with difficulty, to keep her face straight and listen attentively as Kerr went on. "The old fellow . . ." Kerr smiled apologetically . . . "—he seemed about ninety to us kids—he insisted that all the new theory was hogwash."

His smile was pure joy to her, Amber thought.

"He insisted so much that we studied it all the harder. To prove him wrong, you see." His laughter invited them all to join his amusement at this unforeseen outcome and laugh they all did.

"It was actually because of him that I got into quantum physics and the possibility of alternative realities. Fascinating stuff."

Amber's eyes went automatically to her father and this time he did as she expected. He frowned. "That stuff seems awfully farfetched to me," he said. "I like to deal with things I can understand, that I can prove."

Kerr appeared sympathetic. "That certainly makes sense, sir. But there is proof for the new physics; mathematical proof."

The rest of what he said was lost on Amber. She didn't care how many possible worlds might exist side by side but not touching one another. Or what electrons did or did not do when shot through a hole in a screen, though she saw that her father was impressed by this and her mother was listening avidly. There was only one world Amber wanted, she admitted to herself—the one in which she and Kerr had a future together. And it didn't matter to her in the least how many others might or might not exist.

When Kerr went on to something else, her mother turned to her. "I like that dress, dear. Is it new?"

"Yes. I bought it this week." Amber braced herself for the standard lecture on frugality. To her surprise it didn't come. Instead her mother smiled. "It looks very good on you. When did you start wearing your hair down?"

"Just . . . a couple weeks ago. "I . . . I don't wear it to work that way."

"Of course not. It's down for him."

Though her mother's voice was low and the men were engaged in some deep discussion, Amber felt again the pressure of Kerr's leg against hers and knew that he had heard.

"What are you going to do in Denver?" she asked, hoping to direct the conversation away from herself.

"It's a teachers' conference," her mother explained. "Also we could use a little sunshine. We're not as young as we used to be, you know. We plan to take a few days vacation as well. Just enjoy ourselves."

It seemed to Amber then that maybe Kerr was wrong about one thing. Maybe these alternative realities really did intersect and she had fallen into one of them, one where her parents did not behave at all like their usual selves.

The rest of the evening was like that, like a dream

almost. Her practical, down-to-earth mother laughed and became almost coy under the influence of Kerr's charm. And her dry, pedantic father blossomed into a wit.

After dinner Kerr gave them a driving tour of the city, pointing out such landmarks as the Peabody Hotel and Beale Street before he brought them all back to her rooms.

When they reached her suite, her mother pulled her father inside after her and closed the door. Left alone in the hall with Amber, Kerr chuckled. "I think your parents approve of me," he whispered, his eyes on hers.

"*I* think you're some kind of genius," she replied, stepping into the arms he opened for her. "You made my parents into different people." With her lips against his ear she had no fear of being overheard.

He kissed her throat. "No, love. I merely helped you to see them differently."

She was too much aware of his body next to hers to argue. Besides, what did it matter how they spoke of it? The facts were still the same. She turned her face up to his. They had so little time.

"I missed you, darling," he said. "All week I've been waiting for tonight."

"I know." All the longing she was feeling was transmitted in her whispered comment. "Me, too."

He chuckled again. "One kiss and I'd better go. Or else I might lose your parents' good opinion of me. But listen, call me the first thing in the morning. Right after they leave. Okay?"

"Okay."

The kiss he gave her stirred her to her depths and she stood for a long moment, watching him make his way down the hall, letting her knees stop their trembling before she pushed open the door and went in to face the questions she knew were coming.

12

The next morning was a whirl of activity. She had stayed up late, getting to know her parents all over again, realizing that her childhood perceptions of them had not been completely accurate.

Her father could not accept Kerr's alternative realities. He wanted things he could *see*. The only things he was willing to believe in wholeheartedly were his chemical formulas. If you put the right things together, in the right proportions, you inevitably got the same chemicals. And that was enough for him. He had been willing to concede the existence of atoms and molecules. Those, after all, could be microscopically detected, but beyond that he held to a down-to-earth skepticism. And her mother was right there with him.

Yet what surprised Amber was their unconditional approval of Kerr. Later she saw why. In spite of his unbelievable theories, he was a success. And success was, in its way, tangible, identified by fine clothes, a big car, the willingness to buy dinner for four at an expensive restaurant.

Driving back from the airport near noon, Amber mused on these revelations. It had certainly been an interesting evening. Best of all had been her mother's whispered "Hang on to this one" as they left. What would her parents have said if they had seen the *real* Kerr? Then she had to grant that the part they'd seen had been real. But what about the rest of him? His imagination and his sense of fun? What about the Kerr who liked to dress in black and wear a sword?

To her surprise, Amber burst into laughter. What a shock her parents would have had if Kerr had come to her room in costume! They would probably have thought him mad.

She parked the car and hurried past the office and up the stairs toward her suite. She had considered calling Kerr from the airport and had decided against it. There was such a thing as being too eager. This whole dating business was still new to her and she wasn't exactly sure how to handle it.

She hurried around the corner and skidded to a stop. Sitting nonchalantly on the floor outside her door was Kerr. He got to his feet in one fluid motion, his face breaking into a grin. "There you are. Just getting back from the airport?"

She nodded, unable for a moment to speak.

"Good. I guessed right." He smiled sheepishly. "I couldn't wait, so I called. When I got no answer, I took a chance and came over."

Laughter bubbled in her throat as she ran to meet him, as she hurried into the arms he opened for her. His kiss was short and welcoming. For that brief moment she even forgot that they were standing in the hall.

When he released her mouth, she recalled their position and stepped back a little. "What if my parents had seen you here?" she asked. "What if we'd just gone out to brunch?"

His eyes darkened. "Then they would have seen that I can't keep away from you." His gaze swept over her and her blood warmed. "Listen, love. I've got a great tour of Memphis planned for today. Tomorrow I have to fly out at noon. But before I leave I have a big surprise for you. Right now, though, do you suppose you could unlock this door and give me a proper welcome home?"

When she hesitated, he put on a woebegone look. "After all, think what a good boy I was last night. And I waited all week, too."

Amber gave in. She had only hesitated out of a sense of propriety. She was as eager for their love-making as he was. Fishing in her purse, she pulled out the key. "Very well," she said, trying to keep the laughter from her voice. "But I'll hold you to your word. I want that tour of Memphis."

"You'll have the whole works," he whispered, "including Mud Island." His lips were at her ear, his hands around her waist, as she fumbled with the key. "Just as soon as I satisfy my baser instincts."

She couldn't help it. Her laughter bubbled over as

the door finally opened and they almost fell into her room.

He turned her swiftly to face him, one foot kicking the door shut in a masterly fashion. "And now I have you in my power," he said, his voice low and full of passion.

"Yes." Her hands went around his neck; her body pressed itself against his. "Completely in your power."

For a moment she felt his body stiffen, but then the moment was gone and he was swinging her up into his arms and carrying her toward the bedroom. "I missed you so much," he said. "The week seemed like a year. Two years. An eternity."

He put her on her feet inside the bedroom door and looked around. "It's not you," he said finally. "There should be some ruffles and perfume bottles." He looked at the hotel painting hanging over the bed and sighed deeply. "Such a mundane bedroom."

Amber felt light-headed, dizzy. How did he know she liked ruffles and perfume bottles? A giggle rose in her throat. "Maybe that's because I'm 'mundane,'" she said, confident that he would contradict her.

"Oh, no," he said, drawing her toward the rumpled bed. "You can't fool me that way, Amber-my-love. You are one of the most exciting, exotic creatures alive."

She kept wanting to laugh. "Me? Exotic?" She looked down at the plain, tailored gray pantsuit she was wearing. "Now you're working your imagination overtime."

"Not so, beloved." He cast a critical look at her suit. "It's true that your present attire doesn't do justice to your charms." His fingers went out to the bow at the neck of her gray blouse. "But that's soon remedied." He grinned diabolically as his fingers reached inside her blouse and found one eager breast, its nipple already upthrust to meet his touch.

"I'm sorry I didn't have time to change," she said, desire creeping through her.

His chuckle was warm and earthy. "No need for that." His nimble fingers stripped away her jacket and blouse, unhooked her bra, and laid them all aside. His eyes seemed to feast on the sight of her and he laughed softly. "The best outfit you have," he continued as he slipped off her sandals and peeled down her slacks and panties, "is your oldest. Your birthday suit."

On his knees before her, he ran a trail of kisses across the tundra of her stomach and a shiver ran over her flesh.

When he got to his feet, she smiled at him. "Let me undress you," she said, her hands going to the buttons on his dark shirt.

He attempted a stern look, but the twinkle in his eyes made it plain where his thoughts were. "Mmmmm. But don't dawdle. I have urgent business."

Her hands moved eagerly, pulling away his shirt. She lingered long enough to plant a kiss on his chest before her hands went on to his belt buckle and she eased his pants to the floor. As they fell she saw that his shorts were a fiery red and she looked up, laughter in her eyes.

He grinned. "I thought they fit the occasion," he said. "I'm feeling decidedly wicked."

"Maybe I should leave them on, then," she said, entering wholeheartedly into the spirit of the game.

He tried to frown. "Nothing doing. And if you don't hurry up, I'm apt to explode and you'll be forced to pick little pieces of red shorts off the walls and ceilings."

"Oh, no!" she cried, in mock horror. "What ever would the management think?" And she pulled down the shorts and eased off his shoes and socks.

"That," he said, "is an interesting question." He pulled her to her feet so she stood close against him, and she sighed deeply. It really did seem like years since she had felt the goodness of his body against hers.

"Now," he said, leading her to the bed, "let's see which is better, imagination or reality. All week I've been thinking about this, remembering. If it's half as good as I imagined . . ."

She pressed herself as close to him as she could get, reveling in the way they fit together. "Did anyone ever tell you that you talk too much?"

They kissed then, their tongues intermingling, their bodies aflame. Scant moments later he was inside her and they went soaring over the edge again.

Afterward, lying in the circle of his arm, she thought she just might like to lie there forever. After a while, he stirred. "I promised you a grand tour," he said. "And I'm a man of my word."

"Mmmmm." She snuggled closer. "I don't have much interest in Memphis right now."

His hand captured hers, kept it from drawing lazy circles on his chest. "That," he said, "is a deplorable attitude. There are things on Mud Island that I want you to see." He laughed softly. "Besides, love, there are things even Zonan isn't capable of. And since I want to spend tonight and then tomorrow morning with you, we'd better get out of this bed right now."

She met his smile with one of her own. "All right. You win."

Dressing took a little longer than necessary, since several times they stopped to kiss and once almost went back to bed again. But Kerr persisted and midafternoon found them on the monorail high above the Mississippi.

"What is it you want me to see?" Amber asked, looking out over the city behind them and then turning toward the Arkansas shore.

"There's a very good museum," Kerr said. "Lots of historical stuff. I think you'll like it." He glanced at his watch. "But we want to be at the Peabody Hotel before five. So we can see the ducks. You haven't seen them, have you?"

Amber shook her head. "No, but I've heard about them. You can't live in Memphis long without hearing about the Peabody and its ducks. Oh, look down there. What's that?"

"That's a scale model of the Mississippi," Kerr said. "From its beginnings upriver till it reaches the ocean. We can see it better when we get out."

And they did, leaning out over the side of the tower. Amber marveled at the patience of such an undertaking, all built to scale. She felt Kerr's hand on her elbow. "Let's go," he said. "I want you to see the steamboat."

They took their time, pausing before the various displays of old-fashioned tools and utensils that had been arranged in one part of the museum. Amber enjoyed that, but it was when they left that room and entered the saloon-ballroom of the old paddle wheel that she turned to Kerr with a smile. "Oh, this is elegant. Wouldn't it be great to have a costume ball here?"

"It certainly would." He smiled. "I'm glad to see your imagination is going into action."

They went on, peering into a tiny cabin, going down the stairs to the outside deck, seeing the bales of cotton and the dock, everything just as it would have been, back in that so romantic past.

Amber squeezed Kerr's hand. "This is great; thank you for bringing me."

He smiled. "You're quite welcome."

They left the museum and wandered for a little while through the outer court by the Mississippi model before taking the monorail back to the parking lot and the city.

Kerr consulted his watch. "We should make it to the Peabody in time. I want you to see the ducks leaving the lobby. It's something to remember."

They did make it. In fact, they had minutes to spare.

The Peabody was one of the most elegant buildings she'd ever seen. Amber gazed around her, trying to take it all in. Kerr patted the hand he had drawn through his arm and smiled. "It's okay to gawk. The Peabody is something of a local landmark."

"I can certainly see why."

"It was built in the twenties," Kerr said. "They went

in for this sort of thing then. First you have to see the fountain," he continued, leading her across the vast lobby. It was not a particularly unusual fountain—the higher basin was made of some sort of stone supported by smiling cherubs. But the lower marble basin had a unique feature: a number of live ducks, paddling about with a grand air of command, completely at home in this place of studied elegance.

She turned to Kerr. "They look so regal."

He smiled. "I guess they think they're something special."

One of the ducks, as though echoing his sentiment, quacked loudly, and Amber broke into delighted laughter. She'd been laughing a great deal lately, she realized with a sense of wonder.

Kerr nodded. "Yes. They are special. They march down every morning. They have quarters on the roof. And up again every evening. In fact, they should be going up any minute now."

And then, as though in answer to his words, two uniformed attendants crossed the lobby, unrolling a red carpet as they went. The sounds of a processional march boomed out over the lobby and the ducks lifted their heads and looked around. Then, one by one, they clambered out of the basin and down the steps, and lined up on the carpet. And, following the attendants, they marched out, their waddles amusing, yet in some strange way dignified.

"They're like visiting royalty," Amber said.

Kerr grinned. "Maybe they think the place was designed for them and we're here for their amusement."

Amber laughed. "That's an intriguing idea."

"I have another," Kerr said, dropping his voice to that intimate tone she was beginning to know so well. "But I suppose we ought to eat dinner first. I don't know about you, but skipping lunch drains a man's strength. And tonight I'll need all I've got."

"I never even thought of lunch," Amber said. "But I suppose we should eat. Women need their strength, too."

The look he gave her then nearly made her change her mind and urge him to go right back to her suite. But they had to be sensible, she reminded herself. People couldn't live on love alone. The thought stopped her for a minute. Was it love they felt for each other?

She couldn't speak for Kerr, but she did know how she felt. Kerr Corrigan was a wonderful man. She wanted to get to know him even better. And someday, maybe . . . But that was in the distant future. For now it was enough just to be with him.

They left the Peabody then, finding a quiet little place for dinner that was so nondescript that afterward she had no idea at all what it looked like, or even what it was called. As they walked back to the car he said, "How about if we go to my place? That way I can spend more time with you in the morning. Maybe we'll have breakfast at the hotel on my way to the airport. Okay?"

"Okay," she said, moving closer to him. "Are you going to give me the surprise tonight?" she said, her hand on his thigh.

His laughter was merry. "You'd better put your

hand in your lap," he said, "or we're both apt to get a surprise, like ending up in a ditch."

With a big sigh, she removed her hand. "Well, are you?"

"No," he said, throwing her a glance from twinkling eyes. "Tonight is for other things. Tomorrow morning is time enough for the big surprise."

"You're mean," Amber said, the laughter in her voice contradicting her words. "A bully. I think maybe you're a villain instead of a hero."

"Not me," he said. "Zonan wouldn't dream of being mean. Or a bully. He defends the poor and helpless, you know."

Amber giggled. "And fights for truth, justice, and the American way."

"Yes," Kerr agreed, his voice light. "Just like Superman. And a host of other American heroes. I suppose that sounds silly."

Amber shook her head. "No, it doesn't. The world needs heroes. Now more than ever, I guess. Everything is so mundane." She caught her own use of the word and chuckled. "There's not as much sense of personal excitement as there used to be. When a person felt—however wrongly—that he or she could influence the world."

Kerr's voice sobered. "They didn't think wrongly, just differently. As I said before—it's the attitude that counts. Attitude is everything. But you're probably tired of hearing that."

She wasn't. She wanted to be convinced, now more than ever, that his world, his reality, could become real for her, could become hers. But she couldn't very well tell him that. Fortunately at that moment they had arrived at his place.

It seemed very familiar to her now, and when he led her straight into the bedroom, she forgot everything in the pleasure of being with him.

When the alarm went off the next morning, Kerr had to take his arm from around her to shut it off. She opened her eyes and stretched, turning to face him as he rolled back. "Good morning, love." He kissed the tip of her nose. "You look beautiful in the morning."

She smiled and snuggled into his arms. "Thank you. So do you." She kissed his chest. "Now do I get my surprise?"

He chuckled. "Not if you keep on like that. You're a very distracting woman."

She felt like purring. Instead she kissed him again. She'd lost count of how many times they had reached for each other in the night, but it had been many.

"We've got to get dressed," Kerr said. "I'll take you to breakfast at your place and go on from there."

She was reluctant to leave the warmth of his body, but the man did have to eat. And she sensed a seriousness under his banter that gave her a little concern.

A short while later, across the breakfast table from him, Amber sipped the last of her coffee. She was aware of a rising tension in Kerr. Something *was* worrying him. She leaned forward. "What's wrong?"

His smile was sheepish. "I'm not as brave as Zonan, I guess. He could have pulled this off so easily."

"Pulled what off?" She was getting really worried. His tone was so strange and she had never known him to be so nervous.

"First, I have something to tell you." He paused and looked worried. "I'm being transferred to the West Coast. That's why I've been gone so much the last few weeks."

"Transferred." The word sank like a stone into her stomach. She reached for hope. "But you'll be back here sometimes."

He shook his head. "No, Amber. There'll be no reason for that. I start the new job tomorrow. The movers will be in to pack my things. A friend's going to pick up my car at the airport. He's buying it. I won't be back at all, except maybe for next year's convention."

"Next year?" She knew she was stupidly repeating his words, but she couldn't stop herself.

"Yes, Amber. Next year. But listen." His eyes searched her face anxiously. "It's going to be all right. You can come with me."

She knew her mouth had fallen open, but she couldn't seem to close it. The room swam around her.

"I know it's early yet," he went on. "I wish we'd met sooner. But I think we've got a good chance even so." His eyes clouded. "For God's sake, say something."

"I . . . don't know what to say," she finally murmured. It's Andy all over again, the voice in her head shrieked. He just picks up and moves and expects you to go along. You have rights, too, you know. You can't leave your job. You know you can't leave your job.

She said it aloud. "I can't leave my job."

For a moment his eyes showed his pain; then he spoke. "You can get another job."

That's easy for him to say, the voice in her head raged. He doesn't know what it's like to be hungry, to be cold, to be alone in a world of hostile strangers.

"I'll find us a nice place," he continued, as though she hadn't said what she had. "You can wrap things up here and then come out."

"I can't." She didn't know where the words came from. She didn't want to say them. She wanted to be with Kerr. Forever. But the same dead voice went on repeating "I can't. I can't."

For a long moment he stared at her, his face set in grim lines. "Well, then," he said finally. "That's that. I guess I made a mistake. I thought you loved me. I thought you'd begun to see that the world could be bright and beautiful. But no!" His voice began to rise. "You have to go on living in your selfmade darkness. Well, if you want to suffer, you can damn well do it alone!" He got to his feet with such violence that his chair almost toppled over and several people at nearby tables turned to stare. "Good-bye, Amber. Thanks for nothing."

He was gone then and all she could do was sit there, paralyzed by her agony and a terrible sense of loss. Why? Why hadn't she said yes? Why hadn't she taken the risk? she cried to herself. And the caustic voice in her head replied in acid tones. Because you knew; you knew it wouldn't work. It would end up wrong. Just like Andy.

13

The days passed, each one seeming a century long, each one without a word from Kerr. The nights passed, too, but they were even longer. Amber took down the Boris calendar, and the picture of Pegasus, and packed them away. Even looking at the spots where they had hung brought tears to her eyes.

She threw herself into her work, staying late in the office every evening, then walking the corridors till the wee hours of the morning. But nothing helped much. Even physical exhaustion only gained her a few hours of sleep and that was inevitably full of dreams of Kerr.

Finally, one sleepless night, she admitted the truth to herself. She had made a terrible mistake. She should have uprooted herself and gone with him. Her job meant very little to her now. It had always been a substitute for the love she really wanted.

If only she knew how to find him, she thought in the darkness of that night of honesty, she would go to him; she would prove to him that she could live in his reality. She would make him see.

Exhausted by her efforts to think of a solution, she fell asleep, knowing only that she had to find him, someway she had to find him.

She was still puzzling over how when she went to her office the next morning. Should she write to him at his old address, hoping the letter would be forwarded? That would take so long and she wanted to be in touch with him right away.

But duty called and she forced herself to attend to the weekend mail.

And there it was. Almost like an answer to her cry for help. The notice of the Roc-Con. Little Rock's science fiction convention. She had been receiving the science fiction newsletter ever since Mem-Con. Her eyes scanned it quickly and stopped. There was going to be an auction of Boris Vallejo's art, she read, her heart pounding in her throat. A private collector had donated several pieces for the auction, among them a cover illustration called "Auburn-Haired Warrior Woman."

Amber's heart threatened to climb out of her throat. That was it! That was the painting Kerr had had hanging in his bedroom, the one he said looked like her. Her thoughts flew. Surely he would be there to oversee the sale of his favorite painting.

She checked the date again. Two weeks away. Would she have time? But her mind was already made up. She reached for the phone. She was going to Little Rock to seek out Kerr. He might have changed his mind by now. He'd been gone a whole month. But she didn't care; she couldn't let that stop her. She was going and she meant to confront him, to ask him if he still wanted to share his reality with her. That way at least she would know.

Two weeks later Amber stepped back from the mirror in the Little Rock hotel and put her hand on the hilt of her sword. At first she had felt silly, posturing in front of the mirror in the costume she had dug from the back of her closet. But she was determined to go through with this and she certainly didn't want to trip herself up with a sword at the crucial moment, the sword that was meant to convince Kerr that she was ready to share his world.

It would take all her courage to face him. He had every right to be angry with her. She'd refused his most precious gift; refused to share his wonderful reality.

She examined herself once more and nodded. There was nothing more to be done. Every part of the costume matched his. Even the sword was like the one she remembered him wearing.

She glanced at her watch. They would be gathering now, the conventioneers, for the costume contest and the masquerade ball that followed. Tugging nervously at her cloak, she moved toward the door.

The large room set aside for the contest was already half full of people. Amber's heart turned over twice at the sight of a dark head. But it wasn't Kerr's. Could it be possible that he hadn't come? That he was selling his paintings because he wanted to forget even about the art he loved?

She moved slowly toward the center of the room, her eyes searching, always searching for the familiar dark figure they longed to see.

Her heart rose up in her throat. There he was! At the other end of the room, his back to her. She was halfway there, threading her way through the clusters of people, her eyes always on him, when he moved slightly, revealing the person he was talking to.

Automatically her hand went to her sword. He was talking to a woman. Her sable hair was arranged artfully under the white mantilla that framed a pale face of ethereal beauty. But the black Spanish gown disclosed too large an expanse of white bosom and the scarlet nails on the hand that grasped Kerr's arm matched the brilliant hue of her lips. Huge hazel eyes that smoldered with desire gazed up at Kerr.

Amber didn't stop to think any further. She pushed her way through the people, unaware that the expression on her face was actually ferocious. She had almost reached them now, reached the man she loved and the woman who was trying to take him away from her. She forced a smile onto her face and pitched her voice low and throaty. "Zonan-my-love. There you are."

She saw his shoulders stiffen slightly and she almost lost her nerve. But as he began to turn toward her, she brushed aside that threatening red-nailed hand and flung herself into his arms, careful of her sword. She couldn't bear to look into his eyes, not yet. But she wound her arms around his neck and pulled his mouth down to hers. For one terrible, heart-lurching second there was no response, but then his tongue touched hers, his arms went around her hungrily, and he returned her kiss with all the ardor any woman could have wished.

When he released her mouth, she kept one arm around his waist, the one that was not her sword arm. Then she turned toward the woman, whose face was now at least one shade paler. "Who's your friend, darling?" Amber inquired in a tone that left no question as to their intimacy. She let her free hand fall nonchalantly onto her sword.

His voice sounded a trifle stunned. "Margarita," he said. "This is Margarita."

Amber extended the hand that had rested on her sword. "I'm Amber. Or rather, Elizabeth. Pleased to meet you." She hoped her tone was pleasant. "How nice of you to keep my man company till I got here."

A flush spread over Margarita's white cheeks, but her composure remained intact. "Yes, of course. Well, I have some people to see. Nice talking to you, Zonan."

"Yes, yes. See you."

He sounded like a man in a daze, Amber thought as she watched the senorita stroll away with a decided roll to her voluptuous hips. "She certainly does advertise," she murmured. "And well." Then, taking a deep breath, she turned to Kerr. He was staring down at her, almost as though he'd seen a ghost.

"You're looking a little peaked," she said, taking charge. "Let's sit down."

He let her lead him to a chair, but his eyes never left

her face. "I can't believe you're real," he said, still in that dazed voice. "I can't believe it really worked."

Amber ignored the last part. Obviously he wasn't thinking clearly. This was not the time to ask him questions. "I'm really here," she said. "You kissed me, remember?"

He began to look like himself again. "How could I forget? How about an encore?"

"Later," she said and saw his eyes widen at the promise in her own. "First we've got to talk."

"Talk? When I haven't seen you . . ." His hand closed over hers. "Touched you . . . in six long weeks?"

"Talk," she repeated sternly, but her hand returned the pressure of his. "First, who was that woman?"

"Margarita." His eyes were sparkling now.

"What is she to you?"

He shrugged. "Nothing. She means as much to me as that Mr. Holden did to you." His arm went around her waist, pulling her as close to him as the chairs allowed. "But what are you doing here?"

"I had to come," she replied. "I had to see you."

His expression became strained. "I didn't think it would work," he said again. "But it did. It really did."

"Kerr. Zonan. Get a hold on yourself. What are you talking about?"

"I put the paintings up for sale," he said, his face aglow. "I put them up for sale to let you know where I was. I couldn't bear to call or write and have you reject me again. But I thought that if you cared for me at all you'd see the auction notice and come." He took her hand. "But why are we talking about this now? Why are we talking at all? Let's go up to my room."

"Kerr. Stop it! Now, behave yourself." She grew suddenly aware that several pairs of eyes were watching them with amusement. Flushing, she got to her feet and dragged him after her. "All right, come on," she hissed at him. "We'll go to your room. To talk."

"First," he said, grinning down at her. And suddenly it didn't matter to Amber. Let the whole world know that she loved this wonderful man.

"Yes, first," she agreed, pulling him toward the hall. "Now, tell me about our place in . . . My God, I don't even know what town we live in."

"We . . ." he stammered as she hurried him along the corridor.

"Yes, we. You haven't changed your mind, have you?"

She almost couldn't breathe, waiting for the answer to that.

"Of course I haven't changed my mind," he said. "I love you. I want you to be my wife."

Oblivious of the fact that they stood in the middle of a hotel corridor and that people were passing them on both sides, she stopped dead. "Your wife?"

He stopped, too. "Of course. I did propose to you that day."

"No, you didn't."

"Amber, I did. I asked you to come with me."

"But you didn't mention marriage."

He pulled her on, toward his room. "I must have."

"You didn't."

He frowned, trying to remember. "You made me so angry. I knew it was early in our relationship, that you were having a hard time accepting my reality. And I was scared, knowing what I did about Andy. I guess that's why I waited so long to ask you. Till our weekend was almost over. But when you said you wouldn't go, my whole world went black."

He had reached his door and paused to unlock it. "I almost gave up. But then I had the idea about Boris's art. And I decided to try it."

"I saw the notice," she said, following him into the room. "And I hoped you'd be here. You see . . ." She stepped into his arms. "I decided I like your reality. I want to share it with you."

"Is that why you're wearing that sword?" he asked with a grin.

She laughed. "You noticed!"

"I could hardly help it. The darn thing is jabbing me in the stomach."

They laughed together then, unbuckling their swords and laying them side by side across a chair. "I think I'll take fencing lessons," Amber said as he removed her shirt. "You know how to fence, don't you?"

"Yes, I know how." His eyes devoured her, his hands going out to cup her eager breasts. "You can work if you want to, darling. You know that. You won't have to, but I won't stand in the way of your career."

She smiled up at him. "My career was just a substitute," she said. "For the love and family I really want." Her hands paused at his belt buckle. "Children," she cried. "We never mentioned children! Are there children in your reality, Kerr?"

"Several," he said, his face in the curve of her shoulder. "One of each, at least."

"Good, I like that. We can teach them to use their imaginations."

"We certainly will."

They had all their clothes off by now and tumbled naked into the big bed. "It's San Diego we live in," he said, nibbling her ear. "Is that okay with you?"

"I know it sounds terribly old-fashioned," she replied, her lips against his throat. "But I don't really care. I just want to be where you are. To share your reality."

"There's one more thing I want to ask of you," he said, his lips moving across her bare shoulder.

"Yes, what's that?"

His eyes twinkled and his voice was rich with laughter. "Will you promise to save me from other women like you did from Margarita today?"

"You can count on it," she said, her hands moving downward. "Why do you think I want to know how to use that sword? And we can spend long lazy hours in bed while you tell me about our adventures."

"Wait a minute," he objected, capturing her hands. "It's no deal unless you help, too. You've got to use your imagination."

She smiled and snuggled closer. "Agreed. Is there room in our living room for Pegasus?"

His arms clasped her tighter. "You bet. And for my 'Auburn-Haired Warrior Woman,' too. You can buy that one at the auction. We won't need the rest of the paintings. How long will it take you to wrap things up in Memphis and get ready for the wedding? Will you want to go back to Chicago for that?"

"No," she said. "I think I'd like to have it in Memphis." She thought of Betsy's delight. "I have some friends there."

"Me, too," he said. "That sounds good. I can arrange to come back for that."

"I'll want my parents to be there," Amber went on.

"I'm glad about that," Kerr said, kissing her ear. "I like them."

Amber laughed. "You helped me to see them differently. I'd like for them to get a little more fun out of life." She tugged at his beard. "And you're just the person to show them how."

She paused to consider. "I suppose I'll have to give thirty days notice," she continued, tracing the line of his lips with her finger. "They'll need time to find a replacement."

"Thirty days," he groaned. "An absolute eternity. Well, I guess the time will pass. And then we'll be together forever."

"Forever," she echoed softly. "And we'll make our own reality, a bright and beautiful one."

"That we will," he agreed and proceeded to show her just how bright and beautiful it was going to be.

EYE OF THE STORM

MAURA SEGER

A powerful portrayal of the events of World War II in the Pacific, *Eye of the Storm* is a riveting story of how love triumphs over hatred. In this, the first of a three book chronicle, Army nurse Maggie Lawrence meets Marine Sgt. Anthony Gargano. Despite military regulations against fraternization, they resolve to face together whatever lies ahead.... Also known by her fans as Laurel Winslow, Sara Jennings, Anne MacNeil and Jenny Bates, Maura Seger, author of this searing novel, was named by ROMANTIC TIMES as 1984's Most Versatile Romance Author.

At your favorite bookstore in March.

EYE-B-1

Genuine Silhouette sterling silver bookmark for only $15.95!

What a beautiful way to hold your place in your current romance! This genuine sterling silver bookmark, with the distinctive Silhouette symbol in elegant black, measures 1½″ long and 1″ wide. It makes a beautiful gift for yourself, and for every romantic you know! And, at only $15.95 each, including all postage and handling charges, you'll want to order several now, while supplies last.

Send your name and address with check or money order for $15.95 per bookmark ordered to

**Silhouette Books
120 Brighton Rd., P.O. Box 5084
Clifton, N.J. 07015-5084
Attn: Bookmark**

Bookmarks can be ordered pre-paid only. No charges will be accepted. Please allow 4-6 weeks for delivery.

N.Y. State Residents
Please Add Sales Tax

READERS' COMMENTS ON SILHOUETTE DESIRES

"Thank you for Silhouette Desires. They are the best thing that has happened to the bookshelves in a long time."

—V.W.*, Knoxville, TN

"Silhouette Desires—wonderful, fantastic—the best romance around."

—H.T.*, Margate, N.J.

"As a writer as well as a reader of romantic fiction, I found DESIREs most refreshingly realistic—and definitely as magical as the love captured on their pages."

—C.M.*, Silver Lake, N.Y.

"I just wanted to let you know how very much I enjoy your Silhouette Desire books. I read other romances, and I must say your books rate up at the top of the list."

—C.N.*, Anaheim, CA

"Desires are number one. I especially enjoy the endings because they just don't leave you with a kiss or embrace; they finish the story. Thank you for giving me such reading pleasure."

—M.S.*, Sandford, FL

*names available on request